Battlefi...

"'So swallow me, don't follow me
Travelling alone
blue water's my daughter
I'm gonna skip like a stone . . .
And nobody knows me
I can't fathom my stay
And shiver me timbers
I'm sailing away . . .'"

RICHARD SEVERY

BATTLEFIELDS

A Magnet Book

First published in 1987
by Methuen Children's Books Ltd
This Magnet paperback edition first published 1988
by Methuen Children's Books Ltd
A Division of OPG Services Limited
Michelin House, 81 Fulham Road, London SW3 6RB
Copyright © 1988 Richard Severy
Printed in Great Britain
by Cox & Wyman Ltd, Reading

ISBN 0 416 10202 6

'Shiver Me Timbers': words and music
by Tom Waits © Fifth Floor Music Inc,
reproduced by kind permission
of Warner Brothers Music Ltd

For Jann, *who found me just in time*

1 'This thing here in front of you is a field,' said Jerry. Roly stared in a puzzled way at his pointing finger. They were sitting on top of a castle of empty tea-chests outside the Gatehouse.

'Now, this drive leads to the big house. You can see the chimneys poking over those big trees. We're not allowed up there. It's private, Roly. Understand?' Roly glanced up at him. He didn't look away when you stared at him directly, like most dogs, but returned your gaze. It was a look of calm intelligence.

'You know, Roly, I believe you understand every single word I say.' As he spoke, Roly leapt down from the tea-chests, crouched and sprang clean over the hedge. The cat gave a startled yowl and took off up the drive, with Roly in hot pursuit. For a moment Jerry was too taken aback to move. Then he leapt down too and wrenched open the gate.

'ROLEEEEE!'

He vaulted the fence into the field. The drive followed two sides of it. By cutting diagonally across he might be able to head them off.

He reached the bottom of the long slope. The ground here was still soft from all the winter rains and his feet squelched as he ploughed along. He had run out of steam by the time he was half-way up the slope on the other side.

'Pace yourself lad, pace yourself. Elbows in, head up, balls of the feet!' It was the voice of Mr Brady, his old Games Master, tape-recorded somewhere in his brain.

'Long distance running!' he thought. 'What's the use of it? Maybe they won't do it at my new school.' He was ignoring the fact that it was a sport he was really good at.

Jerry reached the fence and flung himself over. Too late! Roly was just vanishing at the far end of a long straight stretch of drive, where it forked at a group of big trees.

'BAD DOG! COME BACK!' The wind snatched up the words and tossed them over his shoulders. He set off at a sprint, his feet crunching on the gravel. He had got into a rhythm now and gradually built up speed, converting the daffodils which lined the drive into thousands of fans waving yellow flags, and the wind in the trees into faint but tremendous applause.

There was a volley of barking up ahead. Jerry began to feel a bit nervous and put on a spurt as he reached the bend. He banked to the right, then to the left, and skidded to a halt.

This was his first view of the house called Battlefields. It stayed clear like a photograph even after many other experiences had made it look quite different in his mind. It was a huge rambling place built of limestone, turned at an angle so that it looked out over many miles of rolling countryside. The gravel drive swept round in a great arc to a front porch framed with pillars. A sinewy creeper grew up the golden stone to the gables and dormer windows, set in a

8

stone-tiled roof. A flagged terrace fell to a huge lawn, a cedar tree, high walls, and a tennis court. The house seemed to sit complacently on its bluff, watching him from its many arched windows. So this was where his father was going to work. Jerry felt rather proud, even if his dad was only going to be the gardener.

Something flashed from the rhododendron bushes, across the drive and vanished round the corner towards the back of the house. Fresh barking and Roly appeared in hot pursuit.

'Roly!' He didn't even check. Jerry raced after him.

The path led into a walled garden full of rose-trees and through a small arched doorway into a cobbled courtyard, lined with out-buildings. He had a confused impression of the back of the house seamed with pipes and patched with windows, Roly disappearing through an open door, a dreadful crash and a startled cry.

He leaned against the door-jamb, gasping for breath. Inside it was like a comic-strip frame: a smashed vase, water and flowers all over the floor; a lady staring down at them with hands raised in horror; a cat arched and hissing on the dresser; a dog glaring up at it. The tall lady turned and looked at Jerry. Her face was rather bony, and there was an expression of alarm in her big dark eyes.

'Now for it!' he thought. 'This must be Mrs Packham.'

'Goodness me! How very . . . Oh dear, poor Willoughby . . . but what . . . that is, who are you actually?'

'Jeremy Mills,' he stammered. 'I'm sorry . . .'

'Well, but what a sudden entrance, you quite took my . . . don't hiss like that, Willoughby . . . and what a fierce dog . . . it's a boxer, isn't it . . . but a white one . . . how unusual.'

'It is a boxer,' said Jerry. It was hard to follow what she was saying, she spoke so fast.

'He's not really fierce. Bad Roly. Come here.' The dog sighed deeply and walked over to Jerry. He always sighed when told off.

'Did you say Roly, as in Jam Roly Poly?' she asked.

'Yes'

'But he's not a bit fat.'

'No . . . it's just his name.'

'Oh . . . Well, I've never seen a white boxer before.'

'There aren't many' he said proudly. 'They're usually killed at birth.'

'What? Good heavens! What can you mean?'

'They don't want them to breed. I don't know why. And they're sometimes born blind or deaf. But Roly wasn't. He has a black spot.'

'A black spot. I see. But what are you doing here? Are you delivering the newspaper?'

'No. My dad's coming to work here. We just moved into the Gatehouse . . . Mr Mills . . .'

'Oh! Mills! Of course. I'm so sorry . . . so that's who you are. I've met your father, of course . . . I was going to pop down this afternoon, once you'd got yourselves . . . but how are you settling in? Do you like the Gatehouse? It's small, but . . .Did you say Jamie? That happens to be my nephew's name . . . such a nice name I always think . . .' She had begun to gather up the flowers. Jerry was about to correct her when she looked up sharply.

'Oh, Jamie . . . You won't let it happen again, will you? My husband would be most . . . He won't have it, you know . . . I'm sure you understand . . . Leonard's had a very difficult time . . . he's still in hospital . . . his operation was . . .' Her voiced trailed off. Jerry noticed a flicker of something like fear in her eyes again, as she bent to the flowers.

''Course not,' he said, grabbing Roly's collar, and dragging him so his big paws skidded across the tiles. 'He's ever so intelligent . . . It's his only weakness, cats. They make him go bananas.'

'I see . . . bananas. Yes, quite. Well, dogs will be dogs. I know Brutus can be very . . . that's Leonard's wolfhound. Of course he's getting old, but he's inclined to resent strangers, if you see what I mean . . . Well, so nice to meet you, Jamie . . . Goodbye.'

Out in the courtyard Jerry broke into a run, Roly at his heels. He glanced at the out-buildings, wondering where Brutus might be kept. As he passed one of the stables, a black horse's head peered out at him. The main exit from the yard led back to the drive. He jogged easily down the straight with the wind behind him, giving Roly a long lecture about cats.

They pulled up at a clump of pines on the corner. The ground to the left fell away gradually to the floor of the valley where he could see the glittering coils of a stream. Beyond that it rose again to a thick wood which rolled away into the distance. It was still mostly grey and brown, but misted here and there with colour as if it had been sprayed with cans of olive and rust-red paint, and the trees along the river were flashing silver green in the wind.

He looked the other way, down towards the Gatehouse at the junction where the drive joined the lane. He could see

11

the little window of his bedroom and Wilf, their new neighbour, digging his garden. No sign of his parents. They'd still be getting things straight. He'd had enough of that the day before.

He noticed that the pine he was leaning on was completely dead, struck by lightning, no doubt. 'Dead Pine Corner. OK?' Roly stared solemnly back at him. The dead tree was like a huge sign-post with charred stumps pointing in all directions. He didn't know the names of any places hereabouts. They'd come here from Coventry, forty miles away. He was used to the streets and alleys of the city, where everything is owned and occupied and covered with concrete. Even the city park where his dad had worked was like somebody else's garden, with its carefully laid-out walks and 'Keep off the Grass' notices.

'Come on, Roly – the first thing we got to do is explore that wood.' Roly started up. He never really sat down, but rested on his haunches, as if to be ready for action. But now he paused and glanced back towards the Gatehouse. Jerry was supposed to be unpacking tea-chests.

'Oh, never mind that! Later!' he said, diving through the hedge into a field of spring wheat.

Two fields later and he was in the water meadow through which the river ran. It was too wide and deep to cross, so he turned right, upstream, and walked for about ten minutes until he came to a kind of ford where the shallow water was littered with big stones. Jerry crossed on these, Roly splashing happily through the water after him. Then he headed upstream on the other bank until he came to a track which led up into the wood.

The ground here was soft and smelt of moss.

Now he was over the ridge of the hill and descending again. He came to a barbed-wire fence, crawled through and stopped to listen. Somewhere not far off was the sound of running water. A sudden outburst of barking set him plunging through the thick undergrowth, and out on to the banks of another stream.

He looked downstream, towards the barking. There was an island! He ran down the bank. It was a small rocky island, almond-shaped, jutting high out of the water, which flowed past it in two channels. The banks of the island were fringed with brambles, but the middle was flat turf, and from it grew an enormous pine tree. Roly had got his head and shoulders inside a hole in the bank opposite the island, and was digging furiously. Jerry looked back at the tree. The trunk went straight up as high as a house. The first branch was at least ten feet from the ground. He waded to the island through the shallows below it, climbed the bank and walked round and round the tree trying to figure it out. Once he'd got past that first branch it would be easy – there were branches or stumps at convenient intervals all the way up to the canopy at the time. He examined the trunk. There were no footholds. He walked backwards to the edge of the island, looking up at the spread of branches in the swaying crown of the tree. What a perfect lookout that would be! The pine towered high above the surrounding trees.

Suddenly the ground crumbled. Jerry lost his footing and threw himself forward. He fell, but didn't hit water. He stared around. He was lying in a kind of cave, formed by the great twisted roots of the pine tree. The soil between them had somehow been eroded, perhaps washed away by flood-water. The earth bank curled overhead, except for the hole between roots, where he'd fallen through. A few feet below the lip of the cave the stream ran swiftly over plates of light-coloured rock, maned with weed. The stony floor was dry and just big enough for him to stretch out at full length.

What a find! The ideal den, with a lookout post high above it. The cave was more or less invisible except to somebody on the bank directly opposite. This was a tangle of briars, so it was hardly likely to be discovered. He started making plans. He would clean out the debris at the back and hollow out a little cupboard for his provisions, make a bracken bed, put up some posters on the wall. He could even put out a night-line, and hook a couple of trout for breakfast. Roly's face appeared at the hole above his head, looking surprised.

'Go on, jump,' said Jerry. He took a lot of coaxing. And then he couldn't get out. Jerry had to put him in the stream to swim round. Before leaving, he dragged a whole bunch of twigs and brambles over the hole in the cave roof to hide it. He decided to get hold of a plank to make a bridge over to the island, and a rope to sling over the first branch, so he could climb the tree.

On the way back through the wood Jerry heard hoof-beats, and Roly turned, growling softly. A rider appeared between the trees, galloping fast towards them on a light-coloured horse. He drew aside to let it pass, but the horse was reined up a couple of yards from him. The rider was a girl of about his age. Black hair spilled out from under her riding hat on to her shoulders. Her dark eyes regarded him steadily. He had an odd feeling he'd seen them somewhere before.

'Who are you?' she asked. 'What are you doing here?'

14

'Nothing,' he said, defensively.

'These woods are private.'

'Are they? I didn't know . . . We've only just moved here.'

'Moved where?'

'It's called the Gatehouse . . . over there.' He pointed.

'Do you mean our Gatehouse?'

'Yours?'

'Well, not mine, my grandfather's to be exact.'

There was a silence. They looked at each other. Jerry remembered the eyes – they had the same penetrating look as Mrs Packham's.

'They're both white,' he said, to break the silence.

'Pardon?'

'They're both white, the dog and the horse.'

'It's not a horse,' she said coldly. 'It's a pony. And it's called "a grey".'

'Oh.'

Then, as if regretting her words, she smiled suddenly down at him.

'I don't suppose it matters,' she said. 'Goodbye.'

She was off in a flurry of hooves, leaving Jerry to wonder what it was that didn't matter, and feeling, at the same time, that it did.

2 'And just where do you think you've been?' His mother's voice was stern.

'Hoot toot! Is that any greeting for a weary lad, the noo?'

'Talk sense. Where have you been?'

'Wheesht! Haven't I bin hob-nobbing wi' the gentry o' these parts, and traipsing the woods and moors for to get you these to bring a sparkle to your eye, wee mither.' And he took some bluebells he'd found on the way home from behind his back and waved them in her face.

'Jerry!' Her eyes did sparkle, and the lines of worry at their corners turned for a moment to lines of laughter.

'I went after Roly. It's great round here! Oh, listen, Mum,' (he had dropped the Scottish accent in his excitement), 'I found a fantastic place, an island in the river . . . I'll need a rope and a plank . . . Roly led me to it really. And what I thought was, you know how Roly can find people when you say their names, well, if I'm in the den and let's say I decide to stay there all day, I could fix a note to his collar saying what I'd like for lunch, such as peanut butter and jelly sandwiches, and say, 'Find Mum'

16

and he'd come back here, and you'd read it and know I was OK, and then you could make the sandwiches and put them in a little box, tie it to his collar and say, 'Find Jerry' and let him carry them back to me.' Jerry's mum stopped looking for a vase and stared at him.

'What?'

'It's perfect for fishing too,' he went on, ignoring her. 'By the way, have you got a rope?'

'A rope!?'

'Yes, a strong rope . . . about twenty feet long.'

'What are you catching . . . whales?' He stared back at her.

'Whales?' Suddenly they both burst out laughing.

'Fetch me a couple of milk-bottles,' she said. 'Goodness knows where the vases have got to.'

Jerry drank a bottle of milk from the fridge and filled it with water at the tap. Then he caught sight of Roly's panting face and poured the water into his bowl. He refilled the bottle and marched stiffly across the room.

'Flower-arranging lesson one . . . BLUEBELLS,' he intoned in his Gumby voice. He seized the flowers. 'Break off the stems . . . and put them in a milk-bottle . . . NICELY!' He jammed them in so hard that water shot up into his face. He staggered back, gasping and spluttering.

'Serves him right,' said his dad, coming in at that moment.

'Look what Jerry's brought,' said his mum.

'Very nice,' he said drily. 'Where did he get them?'

'I *am* present, Father,' said Jerry. 'This is me, standing here. You may ask me directly.'

'Ay! You're here now the work's done.'

Jerry ignored this.

'I found them at the margins of a wood: 'Ten thousand saw I at a glance, tossing their heads in merry dance.' They were wild.'

'So will the owner be when he finds out.'

'Why?'

'Because those woods belong to somebody, no doubt.'

'I don't suppose they'll miss a few,' said his mum, pouring out a cup of tea.

'Just don't let them catch you, that's all.'

There was a sudden rapping at the door. She went to the window.

'It's only Wilf next door,' she said, going out. Jerry heard a gruff voice asking if they needed anything and a few moments later Mrs Mills came back in followed by Wilf.

'. . . everything we need, I think, thank you,' his mum was saying. 'It's just finding it, that's the problem. The house feels a bit damp, but we'll soon have it aired.'

'Well, it would do,' said Wilf, nodding to Mr Mills and Jerry. 'It's been empty most of the winter. The last fellow left . . . sort of sudden, like.'

He was quite an old man, white-haired, with a weather-beaten red face and sea-blue eyes. 'Just like the flag,' thought Jerry. 'Red, white and blue.' He was still strong-looking though. There were blue snakes tattooed all the way up his muscular arms. 'Oh, thanks!' He accepted a cup of tea and sat down.

'Yes,' he went on. 'They couldn't get anyone to take it on, not from round here anyway. He had me running round like a ferret, doing two jobs at once. I'm only supposed to do the stables, see, part-time, but he had me doing all the

18

gardening, and odd jobs too. I'd have been in hospital before him, I reckon, if he hadn't gone in first.'

'What's been the matter with him?' asked Jerry's dad.

Wilf grimaced.

'Knees' he said after a pause. 'He's had artificial knee-caps put in. But summat went amiss. They were forced to operate again – it was touch and go for a while.'

'He's all right now though?'

'Oh, he's right enough, by all accounts. Except he'll be on sticks for a few months and he won't like that. He's a terror for hunting and he's missed the whole season as it is. They've kept on the horses, but I doubt if he'll ride again.'

'Wouldn't that put you out of a job?' Wilf shook his head. He took out a cigarette and lit it.

'Mrs Packham rides,' he said, 'and Miss Amelia, when she's here.'

Jerry pricked up his ears.

'When's he coming out?' asked Jerry's mum.

'Tomorrow afternoon. And there's a shindig at the weekend, sort of coming home party. All his old cronies from the Admiralty. I expect we'll be roped in to help.'

'He was something big in the war, wasn't he?'

'Oh yes . . . He had a Destroyer, you know, submarine chaser. He was a marked man to the Germans by the end of the war – he'd knocked out so many U-boats – but they never got him, he was too wily.' Wilf chuckled. 'Aye – he had a great war. Trouble is, he's still fighting it . . . Eh up!'

This exclamation was caused by Roly. He had begun to curl his lip back and sniff in a disgusted way when Wilf lit his cigarette. Then he had padded up silently while he was talking and, with a quick tap of the paw, knocked the

19

cigarette out of his hand.

'Well, I'm blessed!' The old man stared in astonishment as Roly licked the hot end to put it out thoroughly. Mrs Mills hurriedly picked up the mangled remains.

'I'm ever so sorry, Mr Sedley,' she said. 'Jerry, call that dog off.'

'Come here, off,' said Jerry. 'There's a good dog.'

'That's just what he isn't,' said his dad. 'We don't know why he does it, Wilf. He's never been trained. I've known him chew up a lighted cigar. There's no sense to it.'

'It's his only weakness, Mr Sedley,' said Jerry. 'He worries about cancer.'

'Jerry!' cried his mum. Wilf shook his head and chuckled.

'Well, it were worth a cigarette to see him do it. You ought to put up a No Smoking sign.'

'He's a right mad-head,' said Jerry's dad, fondling Roly's ear.

'Did he get that cat this morning?' asked Wilf.

'Oh no,' said Jerry. 'He never bothers to catch them – he just likes the chase. He nearly got a mongoose in the wood, but it shot up a tree.'

'A mongoose! What kind of a mongoose?'

'Grey, with a bushy tail. It was out looking for snakes.'

Wilf roared with laughter. 'That's never a mongoose! It were a grey squirrel you saw.'

Jerry grinned innocently. 'Is that what you call them round here?'

'He's new to the countryside,' explained his mum. 'We all are really, though Vic spent some time on a farm in the war, when he was a boy.'

20

'You've come at the right time of year. Did you find any birds' nests?' he asked Jerry.

'They were all last year's.'

'We'll, what do you think the birds are doing this year? Going on strike? There's plenty of nests about, if you know where to look.'

'Hey – would you show me, Mr Sedley?'

'Certainly. And call me Wilf, if you don't mind. I'll tell you what,' he said to Jerry. 'I'll meet you by the front wall at six o'clock tomorrow morning. Right?'

'Right!' said Jerry.

'If I get there first, I'll put a stone on it. If you get there first, you knock it off. Right?'

'Right! . . . What?!'

But Wilf only grinned.

It was still dark when Jerry opened the front door next morning. A wave of birdsong hit him. There had been rain in the night and the air smelt green and rinsed. He looked up to Dead Pine Corner. The trees were black against a sky still midnight blue. Along the eastern horizon opposite the house there was a rolling bank of cloud, just turning grey. It was chilly. He zipped up his jacket, and peered at the front wall. There didn't seem to be a stone on it. He still hadn't quite figured out what Wilf had said, but he put a stone on the wall anyway, and walked round to the back garden.

The Gatehouse had been divided into two at some time, but there was no division in the garden, except a concrete path running down the middle. Wilf's part was neatly cultivated in sections, with rows of vegetables already coming up and not a weed in sight, whereas their half had a

21

neglected look. Wilf was standing in his doorway, golden light from the kitchen spilling round his bulky frame.

'Hello, young fellow,' he greeted Jerry. 'You can get up then.'

Jerry rubbed his eyes. 'Not this early usually.'

'It's the best time of day, though I didn't think so at your age. When I were a youngster like you,' he went on, 'we used to be up at four in the morning. Do you know why?'

Jerry yawned. He'd heard this sort of question before. But Wilf surprised him.

'I'll tell you . . . to get into bed with our mother. See, father used to be up at four, rain or shine, to get the horses ready for the day's work in the fields. There were six of us lads. There we'd be, listening at the door, jockeying for position, to make the dash for her bed as soon as he'd gone. To get the warmest place, you see. We had to fix up a rota in the end, to save arguments.'

Jerry laughed.

'I still wake at four mostly – but I don't go back to sleep these days. Seems like the older you get, the less you need.'

'Is it OK if I bring Roly?' asked Jerry.

'I should put him on a lead, so he don't run on ahead and fright the birds. You see, one of the things you got to do is watch where they fly out.'

Jerry fetched the dog and they set off up the lane in the half-light. Wilf beating the hedge here and there with his stick.

'You're lucky to hear the dawn chorus,' he said. 'Do you know what it means?'

'No.'

'Well, every bird's got its own bit of garden, like, and

22

they're all sitting there shouting, 'This is mine – keep off'. It's a pity we don't sound so nice when we shout, 'Keep off', isn't it?'

'Perhaps we do – to the birds.'

'I doubt it,' said Wilf. 'Now – here's the sort of thing . . .' He began peering into a thicket in the hedge, poking branches aside with his stick. Jerry looked at the horizon. There was a red band across the sky now, like an electric ring, and the cloud-bank was fringed with gold.

'There!' Wilf exclaimed, beckoning. The nest was so tiny Jerry could hardly see it – a ball of moss under a hollow tree-stump. He felt inside with one finger. There were four eggs like little warm pebbles in a cocoon of fur. He rolled one out into his hand. It was minute.

'There she is!' The angry wren was hopping from twig to twig, chatting loudly, tail sticking straight up.

'Shall I keep it?'

'I shouldn't. There's only half the birds there used to be as it is, what with all these chemicals they're using nowadays.'

Jerry carefully put it back. 'Did you take eggs when you were a boy?' he asked.

'That I did. Moorhens' mostly.'

Jerry was puzzled. 'Why did you want to collect moorhens' eggs?'

Wilf chuckled. 'I didn't collect 'em – I ate 'em. A few of those for breakfast'd set you up for the day.'

'Oh! What do they taste like?'

'Not as strong as a duck's but rich, you know. Better flavour than a quail's egg, in my opinion.'

'What do they look like?'

'They're like little black hens, with orange bills. Water-birds. They nest in reeds. We used to get them out of the nest with a spoon tied on the end of a stick.' Wilf was puffing a bit and slowing down. 'How d'you suppose we carried them home?' he said.

Jerry frowned. 'In your pockets?'

Wilf laughed. 'I don't think we had pockets! Any road, we used to carry them in our mouths, one in each cheek. It were the safest way. Now then, *you* can do a bit of work. Can you hear that chirping?' He pointed to a place in the hedge which Jerry searched. It was bare of leaves but clotted with dead twigs and brambles. Suddenly he saw it. A woven cup with baby birds in it. At the sound of the rustling twigs they craned up blindly, their mouths wide as shopping bags.

The rim of the sun was just gilding the cloud-bank and sending rays as rich as egg-yolk across the tree-tops. Jerry always remembered that early morning walk. Wilf found three more nests, conjuring them up like a magician pulling rabbits out of a hat.

Jerry reached a stile on the left where a footpath led off across the fields.

'Hey! What's that shining?' he called back to Wilf. As the sun drew clear of the clouds the field suddenly shone like polished gunmetal. He hopped over the stile to investigate. 'Spider's web!' Filaments of web were stretched from blade to blade. They covered the entire field like a net, shimmering for a moment in a shaft of sunlight.

'Billions of them! Look!' he called again, but by the time Wilf got there the sun had gone.

'I've seen it many a time,' he said, leaning on the stile, out of breath. 'That's the battlefield there.'

'What battlefield?'

'The one the house is named for . . . Battle of Burford . . . In the Civil War.'

'Burford! That's where I'm going to school . . . but it's miles away.'

'Aye – well, this is where the battle started, by all accounts . . . but they ran through that wood over there . . . Ducklington Wood . . . and ended up in Burford. Have they taught you owt about the Civil War?'

Jerry frowned. 'Roundheads against Cavaliers. The Roundheads had short hair and the Cavaliers had long hair.'

Wilf stared at him. 'Well . . . it weren't just skinheads and hippies, you know,' he said, shaking his head. 'Any road, this battle was Roundheads against Roundheads, and it weren't any too civil. See what you can find out about it. I'll give you a clue. There's summat in the church at Burford.'

Jerry looked across the valley at the distant wood. 'Is that wood private?' he asked.

'Well, most of it belongs to the Big Chief. This path we're on runs right through it, and it's a public footpath. He wanted to close it down, but he couldn't. It's been used ever since I were a boy.'

So Amelia had been wrong to say he shouldn't be in the wood. He'd been on the public footpath when they met. But she hadn't actually said he shouldn't be there. She'd said the wood was private, which was perhaps a different thing. He remembered the barbed wire fence he'd gone through.

25

Maybe that was the edge of Captain Packham's land, in which case his island was outside it.

The dew was burning off the grass like white smoke. A small bird rose vertically, as if pulled up on a string, and mounted steadily into the sky singing loudly.

'That's a skylark,' said Wilf. 'If you can find one of *their* nests I'll give you ten bob.'

'You mean 50p?' asked Jerry excitedly.

'Same difference. Don't get excited. My money's safe. They're near as difficult to find as a cuckoo's nest. I've only ever found one, and that was by accident.'

'I'll watch where they land.'

'They're up to that one. They come down miles from the nest and run along the ground like mice.'

'Well, I'll have a go.'

'All you want is patience and time. I've got the patience, but I'm running out of time. Which reminds me. I'd best be getting along. Miss Amelia will be wanting that pony, no doubt, and the Big Chief's coming home this afternoon. He'll want everything ship-shape, and then it won't be right.'

Jerry spent hours, later that morning, watching the larks rising and falling like musical yo-yos, running out at intervals to check likely-looking tufts and tussocks for nests. He didn't find one, but Roly caught several field mice.

After lunch he cadged a length of good nylon rope from Wilf and went back to his island. He tied a loop in one end of the rope, threw it over the lowest branch of the pine, made a noose and pulled it tight. It was a simple matter then to climb the rope hand over hand, walking up the trunk, and once on the branch he could make sure nobody followed by pulling up the rope. He climbed rapidly to the top and found a notch of branches which was as good as an armchair.

It was a fantastic view. On one side was the wood, splashed here and there with brilliant green, rising to the ridge, the direction from which he'd come. But the stream was on the border of the wood, and he could now see over the fringe of trees to a patchwork landscape which rolled away towards distant hills. The nearest field was pure yellow with dandelions. In the middle distance a line of trees and the occasional flash of sun on metal indicated a road. He looked down and without realising it, gripped tighter to the branch. He was so high that Roly looked like a toy version of himself. He could see the whole island and the stream parting to flow around and joining again below it. Suddenly he knew what it was.

'Hey! Roly!' he yelled down. The dog peered up into the sky, wondering where the voice was coming from.

'It's a ship!' Yes. The island was shaped exactly like a ship. The cabin was his cave in the bank. He was in the crow's-nest at the top of the swaying mast. He closed his eyes. The tree creaked faintly like the timbers of a great ship, dipping through a choppy sea, and the wind rushed through the pine needles with a hissing sound, which reminded him of pebbles sucked backwards and forwards by breakers on a distant beach. He opened his eyes and felt slightly dizzy. He was poised so high above the deck that he seemed to have no connection with it, as if he was rolling towards the point where the ship would heel over and sink like a stone. He stood up. His head cleared. He took a deep breath.

'Explorations!' he yelled down at Roly. 'Ratskulls! Purple Emperors! Great big hairy caterpillars!'

The dog peered up at the shouting tree with a puzzled expression.

'Haystacks! Tiger moths! Bats! Bottle-dumps! Holes in the ground!'

This was more interesting! Roly began to wag his stumpy tail and bark in agreement.

'Sticklebacks! Owl-pellets! Metal detectors! Frog-spawn! Dinosaur bones!'

Roly was now running round and round the tree barking furiously as Jerry slid down. He had decided to explore the wood really thoroughly. But before doing so he maddened Roly further by swinging to and fro above his head on the rope, shouting things like 'Rabbits!', 'Squirrels!', 'Mice!', 'Dinner!' and 'Cats!'

Later, following a tributary of the river, he found a hidden pool in the wood.

'Aha!' he said, frowning at the stagnant water. 'A likely haunt of the Natterjack Toad.' He began to walk round the pond, hands clasped behind his back, peering short-sightedly into the mass of pale broken reeds.

'Ze Primeval Soup, Herr Roly,' he went on, 'from which has evolved ze rich diversity of life as we know it today. In one square cubicle of zis black slime we can find millions of little animals competing for zair very lives!' Roly trotted after him importantly, then suddenly barked at something in the reeds. There was a splash and flurry of wings. A black bird with a bright orange beak flapped across the pond, chak-chaking with annoyance. Jerry recognised it from

28

Wilf's description. A moorhen! And now he could see the nest, a little raised platform of rushes on the edge of the clear water.

The question was – how to reach it. There was no firm ground. The area between himself and the nest was just black mud with clumps of dead reeds sticking out of it. In the end he decided there was nothing for it but to wade out. He took off his shoes and socks.

'Ze intrepid scientist has no fear of ze leeches which infest zees parts,' he said, hopping and squelching from one tussock to the next. 'He will carry a box of matches and simply apply some flames to zair . . . yikes!' He had slipped and sunk into the swampy ground, when almost within reach of the nest. He crawled forward on hands and knees. There were eight eggs! Cream, splotched with chocolate, about half the size of a hen's egg. He took three, popped them into his mouth, and struggled back to the bank. He hauled himself out and stood, dripping with foul-smelling mud. Roly took a couple of licks, but backed away sniffing in disgust. Jerry removed the eggs from his mouth.

'Zees are ze secrefices of ze modern explorer, Herr Roly,' he said pompously. 'A little soil which can be removed wiz clean water.' But where was the clean water? The pond was no good. Jerry noticed a patch of bog where a trickle of water oozed into the pond. He followed it up a slope hoping to find a clean spring. Instead, he found that the brook flowed out of a pipe set in the hillside. He squatted down and peered into it. The pipe sloped upwards at a gentle gradient. He could only see a few yards into it, but it was big enough to crawl through, and he decided to explore it when he had more time. The water was clear and he managed to wash off some of the mud, though he couldn't get his clothes clean, of course. On the way home he gave Roly one of the eggs to carry, but he instantly chewed it up and swallowed it.

When he got back to the Gatehouse there was an unfamiliar black car parked outside. But he didn't notice it in his excitement. He rushed through the kitchen. There was a little group in the living-room: his mum and dad, Mrs Packham and a man he didn't know, a smallish man on crutches. They swung round at his sudden entrance.

'Oh, Captain Packham, this is . . .' His mum broke off, staring at him. Jerry was besmirched with dried smelly mud from head to foot. The moorhen's eggs made his cheeks bulge like a chipmunk's. He grinned and started to say, 'How do you do,' but it came out as a wordless gobble. He removed the two eggs and held them out.

'Look,' he said proudly. 'Moorhen's eggs. There's a nest by a pool in the wood. I'm going to have them for breakfast.'

'Oh no you're not!' said a quiet acid voice. Captain Packham was staring at him coldly. 'They don't belong to you. You can put them straight back where you found them.'

3 It was like being kicked in the stomach. Jerry stared at Captain Packham, not believing his ears. But he wasn't joking. His mealy discoloured face had gone blotchy and his very pale red-rimmed eyes were fixed on Jerry. He was leaning forward on his crutches, breathing heavily, so that he resembled one of the scrawny young birds Jerry had seen that morning.

'But Wilf told me . . .' he began.

'Shut up, shut up,' snapped Captain Packham. 'Never mind what anyone told you. I'm telling you now. I know that pool. It's on private property. It belongs to Mr Pomeroy. Can you read?'

'Y . . . yes.'

'Well, private means private and keep out means keep out, d'you hear? You've been trespassing on private land. And stealing eggs!' He banged his crutches down hard on the last word. His face was mottled red and twisted with rage.

Jerry glanced at his dad, but Mr Mills looked down in embarrassment.

'And what's *that*?' continued Packham, glaring down at Roly, who looked back at him uncertainly, wagging his tail. 'Nobody said anything about

31

that!'

'But, Leonard,' said Mrs Packham, 'surely . . . when I first discussed . . . I'm sure I mentioned . . .'

'Nonsense!' he interrupted. 'Nobody said anything about it because they knew what my answer would be. However, the harm's done, we'll have to get on with the job, make the best of it, I suppose, madam.' For some reason he had suddenly turned to Jerry's mum. 'I'm sure you understand – I will not have youths running wild on my property, or my neighbour's. Let me see, let me see.' He bent his head and began pulling at his lower lip. Then he looked sidelong at Jerry out of the corner of his pale eyes.

'Do you know the paddock?'

'No.'

'No, *sir*!'

'No, *sir*.'

'Well, get Sedley to show you. It's full of dandelions. I want the heads pulled off before they seed. And every time you pull one off, you say, "I-must-not-trespass". Got it?'

Jerry stared at him disbelievingly. Everyone seemed to be stunned. Mrs Packham was picking nervously at a loose thread on one of her buttons.

'Come on then, Mills,' said Captain Packham. 'Drive me home. There's work to be done.' And he swung out of the door, followed in silence by Mrs Packham and Jerry's dad.

For a few moments Jerry and his mum looked at each other. He had an empty feeling, like hunger, but his mum, reading the shock and disappointment in his face, felt a sharper pain.

'Come along, get those filthy clothes off. What have you been up to? Get off this carpet.' He allowed her to bustle him out of the room and up to the bathroom.

'He's horrible,' said Jerry, staring at himself in the mirror.

'He's not been well, has he? You heard what Wilf said. He's an active man – he's not used to hobbling about on crutches. And what a way to introduce yourself, Jerry – covered in mud from head to foot, with eggs in your mouth.'

'He's still horrible,' said Jerry. 'It's not fair. A whole field of dandelions.'

'I don't suppose it's that big. Don't fret. I'll give you a hand . . . I know. We'll make dandelion wine. I've always wanted to . . . '

The paddock was about an acre of rough grass adjoining the garden containing some huge old sweet chestnut trees. It also contained about half a million dandelions, all in flower. Each one was like a little blazing sun, and after a while Jerry could still see them quite clearly when he closed his eyes. He didn't think 'I must not trespass' though. He thought 'Off with his head', pretending that it was Packham's scrawny head he was snapping off its scrawny stem. And he didn't believe Packham was ill either. He was just one of those miserable strict old fogies that didn't like kids. There were always plenty of them about. Like his old physics teacher, known as the Thug, whose speciality was twisting ears and throwing wooden blackboard dusters.

Jerry could see his dad walking up and down like a guard on patrol, mowing the lawns. He thought he caught sight of Amelia at one of the attic windows, but whoever it was ducked quickly out of sight. Later, a big truck drew up in front of the house and a gang of men started moving about

33

on the main lawn, sorting ropes and hammering pegs. Soon they had some poles erected and began to hoist up canvas.

'That's what I call a tent,' said Jerry, watching the billowing striped awning rising slowly. 'You could sleep about five hundred in that.'

'It's not that sort of tent,' laughed his mum. 'It's a marquee . . . for the reception on Saturday, I suppose. I've got to do a hundred sandwiches.' Jerry looked up.

'But you're not working for them, are you, Mum?'

'No . . . but you've got to show willing. It's a special occasion. Anyway, that's enough dandelions. He can pick the rest himself.'

They had three buckets full of them. When they got home Mrs Mills poured gallons of boiling water over them, to make the wine.

'We can have a party ourselves on Saturday with all this wine,' said Jerry. 'Half of it's mine, don't forget.'

'Get away! It won't be ready by the weekend. It takes months.'

'Oh!' He looked disappointed.

'But I'll tell you what – we'll have a barbecue on Saturday night, if the weather stays fine.'

'Hey! Can we? Hot dogs . . . and toasted marsh-mallows!'

'I expect so, but you'll have to do the fire. I've got to help serve at the reception and I'll be fagged out, I should think.'

Mr Mills didn't come in until quite late that evening. He was having to work overtime to get the gardens looking their best.

'He's thought of something for you to do as well, Jerry,' he said over supper.

34

'Me?'

'Yes. He wants to turn one of the fields into a car-park, there's that many coming, and he asked if you could direct the traffic like and get 'em parked in rows. There'll be something in it for you, he said.'

'I've always wanted to be a car-park attendant!'

'Come on, Jerry – it's no good being bolshy. You want to see if you can get on the right side of him.'

'I shouldn't think he's got one.'

'Now then, son! That's enough!' There was a silence. 'It's Wilf I feel sorry for,' he added.

'Why?'

'He's got a right ticking off for telling you about that nest.'

'He didn't though! I found it myself. It wasn't even on Packham's land.'

'That's what I can't understand,' said Jerry's mum.

'Oh, it's the principle that counts with them,' said Dad.

'What principle?' Mrs Mills sighed.

'The principle of . . . Oh I don't know . . . private property.'

'But he wasn't doing any harm.'

'I told you,' he said in exasperation. 'It don't matter to that sort. He's one of the old school.'

'I know what you mean', said Jerry, thinking of the Thug.

'Anyway, at least you know where you are with him.'

'That's right . . . nowhere!' said his mum. Jerry's dad grew angry.

'Well, what do you expect? That's how I was brought up. That's how it was in them days!'

'But it's not "them days" now, is it?' she persisted.

'Drop it!' he said sharply. Then to Jerry: 'And I think you might apologise to Wilf for getting him in trouble.'

After supper Jerry found Wilf in the back garden, working in his shirt-sleeves.

'Hello, young fellow,' he said cheerfully. 'What's to do?' He showed Wilf the moorhen's eggs.

'That's a moorhen all right – you didn't waste any time, did you?'

'I'm sorry I got you into trouble.'

'Not another word about it. I should have warned you to keep it dark.'

'He didn't give me a chance to explain . . .' Wilf held up his hand.

'It's quite all right,' he said. 'I'm used to it. If I paid any mind to it I'd have been took off in a yellow van a long time ago. What it is, Jerry . . . What it is, you've got to let it in one ear and out the other, see . . . And the quicker it goes through the better,' he added softly to himself.

Jerry nodded. This sounded like pretty good advice to him. He certainly didn't intend to put the moorhen's eggs back after all the trouble he'd had getting them. Wilf showed him how to blow them by making a hole at each end, and he kept them as souvenirs. But he didn't go back to Primordial Pond and on his trips to the island he took care to keep to the public footpath until he was off Packham's land. Mr Pomeroy, who owned the rest of the wood, apparently spent most of his time abroad.

It was a perfect day for the reception – sunny and surprisingly warm for April. Paper signs with the word 'Battlefields' and an arrow had been placed at the turning off the lane and at various points along the drive, with a final one saying 'THIS WAY' at the field entrance. Jerry was instructed to be there by three (although guests weren't officially expected until 3.30pm) and to stand by the gate. There was an opening just inside that led into the next field and he was told to make sure nobody went in there by mistake.

While he was waiting he wondered how to arrange the cars in the field. At first he'd thought of making them spell out a huge word like 'BOO' or 'PIG'. Then he thought they might as well make the word 'JERRY'. He placed Roly in the entrance to the next field to prevent anyone going there and free himself to direct the cars. But when they started arriving he found that most of the drivers ignored him and parked just where they liked.

The fact was that there was plenty of room in the field and he felt useless.

When it seemed that everyone had arrived he began to examine the cars. There were some very fancy ones and he spent some time peering through tinted windows at gleaming dashboards studded with knobs and switches. One particular car attracted him, a metallic blue convertible with the hood down. He wanted very much to sit in the driver's seat, just to see what it felt like. He looked around. The rows of cars simmered in the hot sunshine. There was nobody in sight. From the marquee came the occasional splutter of applause or crackle of laughter.

He hopped quickly over the door and into the soft leather seat. He was faced with a bank of controls like the cockpit of an aircraft. He squirmed down until he could reach the pedals and put his hand on the chunky little gear-stick. The sun glinted on the glass dials. He read the delightful labels: 'Head', 'Master Lock', 'Vents', 'Over-drive', 'Mirrors'. Mirrors! That must mean that the wing mirrors were electrically operated! He gripped the steering wheel, leaned back and closed his eyes. The car smelt richly of warm leather, metal and wood . . .

'I can't hear the engine,' said his companion, resting her head on the back of the seat. 'Are you sure there is one?' Jerry didn't answer. Instead he jammed the accelerator hard against the floor and swung out into the fast lane with a throaty growl of exhaust. The girl smiled and put one of her feet up on to the dashboard. Her long black hair streamed out in the wind.

'Take me away somewhere,' she said. 'Anywhere!'

'I know just the place,' he replied. 'It's an island in a lake. And the lake's on an island, in the sea. We'll make the border by six – and I'll buy you a real Italian ice-cream.'

'Darling.'

He flicked the retro-vamps, spun the wheel and drifted round a hairpin bend. Suddenly he sat up straight. There was a police road-block ahead. So! The Swiss police were in on the frame-up too. Pedro must have sent a laser message by satellite!

'Hang on to your hat,' he said quietly, and braced himself for the most difficult driving manoeuvre of all; a U-turn executed at high speed . . .

'Having fun?' said a voice. He spun round. Amelia was standing behind the car, carrying a drink and a plate of food.

'I just . . .' spluttered Jerry. 'I was just checking the lights. I thought the lights were on, but it must have been the

38

sun reflected in . . .' He tailed off lamely at her knowing grin.

'Well, don't you want it?' She held out the drink. He hopped out and took it.

'Thanks!' It was a fruity drink with a slightly bitter taste.

'What is it?'

'It's a wine cup.' She offered him the plate. It was strawberries in a kind of pastry boat and a cucumber sandwich.

'Strawberries! Thanks!'

Roly came bounding up. He'd been waiting patiently and finally given up.

'You're in luck, Roly,' said Jerry, giving him the sandwich. 'He loves cucumber – he really looks forward to it.' Roly swallowed it one gulp.

'He's funny,' said Amelia.

'He does all kinds of things,' said Jerry. 'He can sing.'

'What do you mean?'

'Listen!' Jerry took a breath and shouted in a high-pitched voice 'Hip Hip'. Roly threw back his head and howled 'Hooooraaay' in the most mournful way imaginable. Amelia burst out laughing and made him do it over and over again.

'He plays football too,' said Jerry. 'We were walking near the football ground in Coventry once, and he heard the whistle go. He was off like a shot. When we got there all the players were on the touch-line and Roly was in the middle of the pitch with the ball. He wouldn't let anyone have it. Wouldn't have been any use if they had.'

'Why?'

'He'd punctured it.' She giggled.

39

'When do you go back to school?' she asked.

'Monday. How about you?'

'I've got another ten days.'

'Ten days! You're lucky!'

'Well, it's a boarding school. They make us work harder in the term.'

'Do they?'

'We have prep in the evenings and chapel and lessons on Saturday.'

'Well, we have homework.'

'But it's not the same.'

Suddenly there was a volley of barking from the direction of the garden. Jerry ran to the end of a row of cars. The garden gate was open. Roly had gone through and met a Yorkshire terrier. He had rushed up to greet this small hairy dog with his usual enthusiasm but it had misunderstood his intentions and was yapping in terror and running round in circles. A lady in a wide-brimmed hat appeared from the marquee and hurried over.

'My poor little Lollie,' she wailed.

Jerry grabbed Roly's collar. 'Sorry,' he said.

'Great hulking brute!' She snatched up the little dog. 'Did he frighten my Lollie-Polly-Doodle-Bug?'

'He didn't mean any harm – it's his only weakness. Bad Roly!' Roly heaved a deep sigh. Jerry straightened up. Swinging furiously across the lawn towards them was Captain Packham. He had a pipe sticking out of his mouth and was very red in the face. Jerry turned away.

'Just one minute,' called Packham. 'Stay there!' They stood watching him approach.

'What's going on here?' he shouted.

40

'Oh, it's quite all right,' said the lady. 'Lollie was very brave.'

Captain Packham pulled up, breathing hard, and leaned on one crutch, taking the pipe out of his mouth.

'What's that thing doing here?' he asked Jerry. 'It's obviously out of control. What the devil is it doing in my garden?'

'The gate . . .' began Jerry. But he didn't get any further. None of them had noticed Roly's lips curling in disgust at the smell of tobacco smoke. With a quick flick of his paw he batted the pipe out of Captain Packham's hand and sent it spinning to the ground.

4 The pipe lay on its side in the grass, smoke curling up thinly from the bowl. Everyone stared. Jerry recovered first. He bent to pick it up, but Roly was too quick. He pounced, grabbed it in his teeth, and ran out of the gate into the field. He stopped by a car and looked round at them impudently, the pipe sticking out of his mouth as if he were smoking it.

'Damn the thing,' muttered Captain Packham, swinging rapidly after him. As he came up, Roly shook his head vigorously so that bits of tobacco flew out. Cursing furiously, Captain Packham dug one crutch into the ground, raised the other and swung it at Roly. Roly dodged easily. There was a splintering crash. The crutch had hit a wing mirror. Captain Packham fell against the car with a startled cry. Amelia gave a kind of snort.

Roly dashed off between the cars. Jerry gave chase, calling, 'Don't worry – I'll get it,' over his shoulder. Roly dodged this way and that and crawled under cars to make it more interesting. Jerry finally ran him to ground under a Range Rover in a corner of the field. He was crouching over the pipe as if it were a bone, panting and slobbering.

'All right, Roly,' gasped Jerry. 'Game's over. Let's have it.' He lay down and crawled under the car. Roly gave a mock growl, picked it up again and started backing away. Then he stopped and looked over his shoulder. Amelia was on the other side, blocking his way out. Jerry took advantage of the distraction to grab the pipe.

'Got it!' He examined it in the half-light. 'Oh no! It's all chewed up.' The pipe was soaking wet. There were tooth-marks all down the stem, and the plastic bit on the end had disappeared. Amelia wriggled under the car to look at it. She gave a little squeal of laughter.

'He'll have a blue fit! You wicked thing!' she said to Roly, who sighed and looked puzzled.

'He's against smoking,' explained Jerry. She stared at him. Their faces were only about a foot apart. Suddenly they both started laughing at the same moment. The situation was so ridiculous. Amelia brushed a tangle of dark hair from her face, leaving a smear of grease on her nose. Jerry bumped his head on the car chassis. He pulled a face and groaned, which set her off in fresh peals of laughter. Suddenly she stopped, her eyes shining.

'I know . . . I've an idea . . . He's got another just like it . . . you stay here and hide, while I get . . . he'll never know . . . I'm sure it's the same sort. Let me have another look.' She reached out for it. Her hand closed over his and a kind of electric shock ran up his arm. At that moment Jerry saw something behind her, out in the sunshine: a pair of shiny tan shoes and the tip-ends of two crutches.

'Come out at once, Amelia,' said an acid voice. 'What are you doing under there with the gardener's boy?'

She snatched her hand away and frowned. Then she

43

grinned at him and wriggled out like an eel. Jerry lay still for a moment, stung by the words. Then he crawled out too, and stood up.

Packham was staring grimly at her dirty face and crumpled dress. 'Inside!' he snapped. 'Get yourself cleaned up. You look disgusting.' She walked slowly off. Jerry held out the broken pipe, but Packham ignored it. He pulled his lips back in a mirthless smile.

'It seems you've got a lot to learn about the way we do things round here,' he said. 'Come with me.'

Jerry called Roly to heel and followed him across the field towards the back of the house, wondering what he was in for now. Packham carried on talking as they went.

'I know about you townies,' he was saying. 'No discipline . . . no respect for property . . .'

'Here we go,' thought Jerry. 'Remember what Wilf said. In one ear and out the other . . .'

He imagined Packham was an old radio set with very poor reception. There was a lot of static interference and another channel kept breaking in with bagpipe music. But odd phrases kept coming through.

Jerry was trying to picture an on/off switch (located somewhere among the remnants of hair on the back of Packham's head) when he realised they were in the cobbled courtyard. Packham swung round, slammed the gate shut and put his head on one side and grinned. There was something in the grin that Jerry couldn't turn into a joke.

'Tie that thing up,' he said. 'I want to show you something.' Jerry tensed up, all his senses alert. He took Roly's lead out of his pocket, fastened it on to his collar,

44

and put the loop over a hook in the wall. Packham threw open the door of one of the stables. There was a sudden pattering of paws and rattling of chain. A huge dog appeared in the doorway. It was a great lanky grey wolfhound, as high as Jerry's chest. Its tail curled upwards as if held in position with stiff wire. Its eyes were hidden in a tangle of dirty grey hair, through which it peered, rolling its great head from side to side. Suddenly it caught sight or scent of Roly and bounded forward with a snarl. The chain brought it up short and jerked its head backwards twisting it off its feet. It scrambled up immediately and pulled the chain taut, baring broken yellow teeth.

'Just stand perfectly still,' said Packham. 'BRUTUS! BEG!' The dog cringed down and grovelled at this command, making small whining noises. He bent down and unfastened the chain from its collar. Jerry glanced nervously at Roly. He was straining forward on the lead, growling softly.

'Perfect guard-dogs. They dislike strangers,' said Packham. 'Watch this. BRUTUS! GUARD!' The wolfhound rose to its full height in front of him, standing with rigid legs, fur bristling and ears back.

'BRUTUS! DOWN!' Now the dog sank on to its belly at his feet, curling its thin mouth back in a snarl. 'D'you see! Perfect control. That's the difference. Dogs have to be trained to obey command, just like soldiers.' He grinned again. 'They have to learn their place, d'you see? I have only to say the word, and he'd tear you to pieces.' The wolfhound began to slide menacingly towards Jerry.

'BRUTUS! KENNEL!' snapped Packham. The dog checked, and half turned towards the stable, but then

45

stopped and looked back at Jerry.

'Kennel!' repeated Packham sharply. Once again Brutus cringed and very reluctantly began to move towards the stable.

'GET A MOVE ON!' shouted Packham, suddenly angry, and took a few paces forward. A crutch slipped on the cobbles and he stumbled. Instantly the wolfhound turned and sprang at Jerry with a kind of grating howl. He jumped sideways, but the jaws closed on the corner of his jacket. Roly barked furiously and flung himself forward. Packham recovered his balance.

'YOU DAMNED BRUTE!' he yelled. He raised one of the crutches and brought it down heavily on Brutus' head. Jerry tore himself away, but even under this blow Brutus did not let go and a piece of cloth was left in his jaws. He raised his great ugly head and stared straight at Jerry, blaming him.

'KENNEL!' screamed Packham, striking him again. Brutus turned and slunk rapidly into the stable. Packham followed, slammed the door on him and bolted it. Then he swung round to face Jerry, his features working, trembling with rage.

'You provoked him!' he shouted. 'You moved! I told you not to move!' Jerry was too stunned to reply. Packham turned on Roly, who was still barking madly.

'SHUT UP!' he screamed, raising a crutch. 'Get that dog out of my sight – and yourself with it.'

Jerry undid Roly, threw open the gate, and ran back to the field where the cars were parked. He felt numb and slightly sick. He could still see the eyeless face of Brutus with its mangy grey fur like bits of used wire-wool, feel the hot breath on his wrist and hear that peculiar grating howl. He walked straight into the post with the 'THIS WAY' sign at the field entrance. He rubbed his shin angrily and looked around. Why had he gone back there? He hadn't even been paid for his work. He kicked the sign savagely. It slewed round so that the arrow pointed into the adjoining field.

'Serves them right!' he muttered. 'Come on, Roly.' They ran back through the fields.

Wilf was sitting on the step listening to the football results on the radio and marking off his coupon.

'Hello, young fellow,' he called. 'Found that lark's nest yet?' Jerry shook his head. Wilf glanced up at him.

'What's up, lad?'

'Oh . . . nothing much.'

'Come on, two heads is better than one. Has summat happened?' Jerry sat down on the step.

'Brutus . . .' he began.

'Brutus!' exclaimed Wilf. 'He was never loose at the party?'

'Nooo . . . It was in the courtyard. Captain Packham took him off the chain . . . he went for me.' Jerry showed the rip in his jacket. Wilf whistled through his teeth.

'He's gone bad. And Packham knows it. It ain't the first time this has happened. Whatever possessed him to take that chain off?' Jerry sighed.

'Something about discipline he said . . . Roly got hold of his pipe and he didn't see the funny side of it.'

'He wouldn't . . . That hound should have been put down years ago. But Packham won't hear of it. Well, well . . . never fret. Don't pay him no mind. Remember . . . in one ear and out the other.'

47

'I tried that,' said Jerry miserably. Wilf put the paper aside and turned the radio off.

'Listen,' he said. 'I'll tell you a story, but it musn't go no further, mind. Years ago, this was. You know the garden seat, the one beside the front door? Well Mrs Packham wanted it painted, brown she wanted it – a sort of khaki. So I paints it up real nice for her and I'm having a cup of tea from the thermos when the Big Chief comes charging out. He's all dressed up for some inspection he's doing, white uniform, you know, gold braid and all that. "What are you doing drinking tea, Wilf?" he cries, "Get me a buttonhole. Staff car was due twenty minutes ago and I'm in a hurry."'

Jerry looked up.

'What's a buttonhole?'

'A flower like, to wear in his lapel. A carnation, it might be, or a rose. Any road, I starts to tell him about the wet paint, but he won't let me speak. "Don't stand there blathering like an old goat!" he says. "Get me that buttonhole and get it quick." "Right," I thought to myself, "Old goat, is it?" I didn't say another word. I went to get the flower, and sure enough, when I get back, there he is, sitting on that garden seat.' Wilf slapped his knee and broke into a wheezy laugh. 'Just then the car rolls up. Up he jumps, snatches the rose from me, and starts rating the driver for being late. I couldn't take my eyes off it. A great khaki-brown splodge on the seat of his pants! Then the ensign sees it too.' Wilf chuckled. 'He knew I knew . . . and I knew he knew I knew . . . but the thing is, neither of us didn't dare say anything about it, the Chief being the sort of man he is. So the ensign opens the door for him and sort of looks at me, and I sort of looks at him, and off he went . . .

to inspect a parade!' Wilf doubled up and Jerry joined in. 'The funny thing was,' he went on at last, 'I never heard a thing about it. I was expecting the bollocking of all time . . . but never a word was said. I sometimes wonder what happened at that parade . . . Any road, when he's sounding off like, I always concentrate on that picture . . . in my mind . . . it works wonders! Helps me control my tongue. Now then, if you're feeling a bit more like yourself, I might remind you that I've been invited to a barbecue at this address tonight.' He looked around. 'But I don't see much sign of it.' Jerry leaped up.

'Oh gosh! I'm supposed to be getting it ready.'

'Come on then – I'll give you a hand. Where are you putting the fire?'

Jerry glanced around. Wilf's garden was limited by being on the corner of the lane, and was almost all vegetables, but theirs extended on the side of the house with a delightful little orchard, hidden by the front hedge, and beyond it a chicken run enclosed by wire. The orchard was set with low hedges and miniature paths winding between the ancient fruit trees. It was here that Jerry wanted the barbecue, but he hesitated. The turf was so fine and smooth it was a shame to burn it. And whose turf was it anyway? Theirs or Captain Packham's?

'That's all right,' said Wilf, following his glance. 'We'll do it gypsy-style.'

'How's that?'

'Simple. You cut out your square of turf, and put it safe to one side. Then you dig your pit and make the fire. When you've finished you fill it up and put the turf back. Nobody's the wiser and you've done no damage to the

49

ground. In fact, you've done it good, with the wood-ash. When my wife was alive, we used to say we could have a kettle boiling in half an hour. How about that?'

'Right!' said Jerry. He and Roly raced off to collect dead wood, while Wilf dug the pit, and by the time his parents came back they had sausages frying over a blazing fire.

'That's a good smell,' said Jerry's dad.

'That's cherry, I reckon,' said Wilf, 'or plum. You can't beat fruit wood for scent.'

'And it didn't cost anything.'

'Nothing's worth nothing but it's free,' said Wilf. They thought about this.

'You can't live on air though,' said Jerry's mum, 'unfortunately. What did you get for doing the cars, Jerry?'

He hesitated. 'Well . . . I got a drink . . . and some strawberries. Roly had a cucumber sandwich.'

'Well!' she looked at her husband. 'I don't call that . . .' He shook his head slightly.

'When are we going to get these sausages then?' he asked Jerry.

'Hot dogs, Pa,' he drawled. 'Hot dogs is what we call 'em down country where I come from.'

'Here we go again,' sighed Mr Mills.

'Come on, be the first Pa on your block to try a Guaranteed Genuine Wholesome 100% Natural Buttered Hot Dog with strings attached.'

'I'll just have a straight sausage, in a bap, if you don't mind, son.'

'A *bap*?? Oh well! Hey, these sausages are all bent. No problem. I'll straighten one out for you.'

He seized a sausage, 'Straighten up and fly right, you

50

hear?' He tried to bend it straight but burnt his fingers and dropped it on the lawn, where it was instantly snapped up by Roly. Mr Mills stared in mock outrage.

'Great! Wonderful!'

'It's his only weakness, sausages,' Jerry explained to Wilf. 'And hot dogs when they're in season.' Jerry collapsed with laughter at this.

'I don't know where he gets it from,' said Mrs Mills.

'It all started with that daft parrot of his grandad's,' said Mr Mills. 'That's where I put the blame.'

This gave Jerry an idea. He grabbed Wilf's spade and fork, which were leaning against a tree, and stuck the handles under his arms. Then he pulled his face into a hideous leer and began to swing up and down under the trees, one leg doubled back at the knee.

'Splice the main-poops, my roaring Top-Gallants,' he wheezed. 'Haul away, Jim lad. We'll have those barnacles for breakfast or my name's not Silver, by thunder.'

'Jerry!' His dad glanced nervously towards the hedge.

'Stand by to go about!' squawked Jerry in a parrot voice, wheeled round and limped back. 'Barbecue for Cap'n, barbecue for ever!'

'Jerry, no!'

He stopped with a hurt expression. 'Shiver me timbers?'

'No!'

'Long John Silver, Dad?'

'NO!' Jerry let the tools fall to the ground, then pretended to suddenly realise he had no support, tottered about and crashed down like a felled tree. His dad had got up and was staring over the hedge.

'What the devil's going on?' he muttered. Jerry jumped

up and looked.

'Oh cripes!' he said.

5 There was a blue car in the field opposite! As they watched, it reached the bottom of the slope and began the long climb up towards the Gatehouse. But it didn't get far. The ground there was sodden with spring rains. The wheels began to spin uselessly and the engine rose to a high-pitched scream. The car stopped, then slid backwards into the hollow. The engine screamed again and two plumes of mud rose from the back wheels, but the car didn't move. The engine stopped. The door was flung open and a man in a pale grey suit got out. He stared all round and rubbed his forehead as if wondering where he was.

'What's going on, Jerry?' asked Mr Mills.

'It was an accident, Dad.'

'An accident! What do you mean?'

'I just sort of hit the sign, and it swung round . . .' Mr Mills stared at him in horror.

'Look!' said Wilf. 'Here comes another one.'

A red sports car had appeared following the track left in the long grass by the first car. It was an open two-seater. A man wearing a flat cap and holding a bottle in one hand was driving with a girl in the passenger seat. The man in the pale grey suit caught sight of them and waved at them to go back. The girl stood up in the car and waved back at him. The driver began to zig-zag down the slope in a slalom, laughing uproariously. The grey-suited man shouted at them to stop, holding up both arms like a policeman. The driver in the flat cap suddenly seemed to realise the situation and slammed on the brakes. But it was too late. The car slewed right round and ran slowly backwards, hitting the blue car with a soft but audible crunch.

'Bloody hell-fire,' muttered Mr Mills. Wilf broke into a wheezy laugh.

'How could you, Jerry?' said Mrs Mills. Jerry felt an odd mixture of alarm and joy.

'I never thought they'd take notice,' he said. 'I just did it on the spur of the moment.'

'On the spur of the moment!' exploded Jerry's dad. 'I don't believe this. I just don't believe it.'

The driver of the sports car had got out rather unsteadily and was peering at the meeting-point of the bumpers, while the grey-suited man was pointing and shouting furiously at him. The lady got out and walked a little way off as if she wanted nothing further to do with the scene, but suddenly she bent down with a cry of disgust, and began hopping about trying to wipe something off her shoe. The flat-capped man suddenly staightened up, shook the bottle he was holding and aimed it at the grey-suited man. A spout of fizzy liquid shot out and hit him in the face. He staggered back, tripped and fell into the grass backwards. A third car appeared at the top of the field; the Range Rover that Roly had hidden underneath.

'No! Not another,' groaned Mr Mills. Wilf made a big

effort to stop laughing.

'It's all right,' he spluttered. 'Those Range Rovers have got four-wheel drive. He'll pull the other two, I shouldn't wonder.'

The Range Rover stopped. Some people got out, staring in amazement as the man in the pale grey suit chased the flat-capped man round and round the two cars. The lady's high-heeled shoes seemed to have stuck in the ground. She swayed backwards and forwards, screaming.

'Jerry!' said Mr Mills. 'I think you'd better go to your room!'

The last thing Jerry saw was the man in the flat cap brought down with a strangled cry by a flying rugger tackle from the man in the grey suit. Later that evening Jerry's dad came up to his bedroom.

'Wilf put in a word for you,' he said. 'It seems you had some provocation for what you did. Why didn't you say so?'

'I didn't have a chance.'

'Well, what happened exactly?' Jerry told him about the incident in the courtyard. His dad was silent for a while.

'He had no business frightening you like that,' he said at last. 'But two wrongs don't make a right. You'll have to own up and apologise.'

'Oh, Dad! Why! I've owned up to you, haven't I? They're not to know who did it. It might have blown round in the wind.'

'No,' he said firmly. 'We've got to keep our side straight. That's the way I was brought up. Own up and take the consequences. It doesn't matter what he's done. We've got to keep honourable.'

'You won't leave me alone with him, will you, Dad?'

'I'll go with you. You can come with me tomorrow morning when I go to work.'

'I didn't mean any harm.'

'I know that, Jerry. But you've got to realise something. Things you do affect my job and our whole position here. Most folk'd laugh it off. But we're not up against most folk. We're up against Captain Packham.'

'I know!'

'This isn't a bad little job, especially when you've been on the dole as long as I have. It's outdoor work, the kind I like, and it's food on the table and a roof over our heads. But if I'm sacked, what happens? We lose job, house, the lot. We'd have to get out in a month. And where'd we go? Back to Sutton Hill. You don't want that, now do you?'

Sutton Hill was a Council estate in Coventry where they'd lived before they moved. Jerry shook his head.

'No, Dad.'

'No. Neither do I. I want to make a go of it and I'm prepared to swallow my pride for all our sakes. He's a difficult man. But remember, Jerry, he's fighting old age and bad health . . . and those are battles you just can't win, in the end . . . Do you understand?' Jerry nodded.

'I just want to keep my head down, get on with my work and draw my wages at the end of the week.' He put his arm round Jerry's shoulders. 'Mayhap his temper will sweeten when his health improves. So let's have no more pranks. Make a clean breast of it and turn over a new leaf.'

'Yes. Just don't leave me alone with him.'

'I won't.'

The weather changed in the night. The next morning the

56

sky was thickly overcast and a cold wind was blowing. Some of the daffodils were already past their best, turning brown and shrivelled at the edges.

'I shall have to dead-head these,' said Mr Mills. 'Now, Jerry, don't forget to call him sir,' he added as they entered the courtyard. Jerry glanced round nervously but there was no sign of Brutus. His dad knocked on the back door and after a while it was opened by Mrs Packham.

'Oh! Mr Mills . . . and Jamie . . . This is an early visit . . . Come in, come in out of the . .. chilly this morning, isn't it?'

'It is indeed,' said Mr Mills. 'Is the Captain in by any chance? The lad has something to say to him.'

She looked flustered.

'Oh dear . . . well, he's not very . . . He had a bad night actually. He gets these . . . depressions . . . . . . was there something I could do?'

Jerry's dad looked rather relieved. 'Well, I reckon it don't make any odds, if you'd take the apology on his behalf like.'

'Apology?'

'Yes . . . go on then, Jerry.'

'I'm sorry about the cars,' he gulped.

'The cars? But I thought you did such a good job . . . getting them all parked so . . .'

'No . . . in the field, afterwards. I . . . bumped into the sign and it swung round and pointed the wrong way, but I never thought they'd all go into that field.'

Mrs Packham stared at him, then suddenly gave a peal of laughter. 'Oh! . . . I see . . . we all thought it was Miles . . . my cousin, you know. He has such a wicked sense of humour . . . and he'd had rather a lot to . . . so it was you after all!' She laughed again. 'It was terribly funny . . . Richard was furious, but there was hardly a scratch on his bumper . . . What a sight they looked when they came in! Absolutely covered in mud . . . Fortunately, Leonard had some spare . . .' She stopped. 'It's very brave of you to own up, but . . . we won't say anything to Leonard . . . it would only upset him . . .'

Mr Mills nodded. Jerry noticed her eyes cloud slightly as she fell silent. He turned to go, but his dad nudged him.

'Oh! Can I do anything to help, Mrs Packham?'

'Well . . . how kind of you . . . let me see . . . yes . . . indeed. Would you bring in the glasses from the marquee? That would be most helpful.'

Jerry said goodbye to his dad and went round to the main lawn. The sky had darkened and spots of rain fell as he entered the marquee. Inside, it smelled of warm crushed grass. The green-striped awning filtered the light, giving an underwater feeling. The ground was trampled and littered with doilies, paper cups and plates. Two trestle tables ran down the sides to an elevated wooden platform at the far end on which was a table, some chairs and a piano. Jerry walked slowly along the right-hand table, feasting his eyes on the vast bowls of fruit and half-eaten sandwiches, cakes and pastries. Many of the glasses and bottles still contained wine. He began to collect them up. He read the label on one of the bottles.

'Hmmm . . . Pimms.' He clasped his hands behind his back and walked stiffly down the table as if inspecting a parade. A vase of flowers had been knocked over, so that they were strewn across the table. Jerry stopped and turned to an imaginary subordinate.

'What's the meaning of this, Pimm?' he said sharply. 'It's an absolute shambles.' Then he stepped sideways and adopted a deferential stance.

'It's the heat, sir,' he replied, in a snivelling tone of voice. 'These men have been on parade for six hours, sir, awaiting the inspection.'

He stepped back, and straightened up. 'I can't help that! What a shower! What unit are they from?'

'Fifth begonias, sir.'

'Prop 'em up against a wall, and shoot 'em!'

'Very good, sir.' Jerry moved on slowly.

'And look at these strawberries. Sinking in their own juice.' He popped one into his mouth. 'They've gone soft. That's the trouble with this damned country.' He came to a cluster of champagne bottles and eyed them critically. 'See these bottles, Pimm,' he said in a low voice.

'Yes, sir.'

'They're half-drunk, on parade – take their names!'

'They're all called Bollinger, sir.'

'Are they, by Gad! We'll see about that. I suppose they think they're being funny.' He picked one up and swigged the remaining drink, then glared at the bottle, eyes watering. 'This one's completely drunk . . . and its label's on crooked . . . Have it flogged.'

'I couldn't flog it, sir . . . it's not worth anything now it's empty . . . HA HA HA . . .'

'I don't wish to know that, Pimm.'

'No, sir. Very good, sir.'

'What's that sniggering?'

'Well, sir, I don't know quite how to put it, but . . .' he

lowered his voice, 'have you sat in anything recently, sir?'

'What the devil do you mean?' he roared back. 'Of course I've sat in things . . . staff cars, aeroplanes, tanks, helicopters, aircraft carriers . . . you name it, I've sat in it. So what?'

'Don't turn around, sir. Just keep facing the men.'

'Why are they falling about like that?'

'It's the heat, undoubtedly, sir . . . er . . . excuse my mentioning it, sir, but had you thought of changing your . . . er . . . dress?'

'Changing my address? Certainly not! I've lived at Battlefields for a hundred and ninety-seven years and I'm not moving now!'

Jerry had reached the platform. With a bound he was up on to it. He swung round and stared grimly down the marquee.

'Now listen to me, you no-good bunch of horrible leftovers. Never in all my years as General Officer Chief of Staff Western Sector 1st Battalion High Command 5th Dragoon Gherkins have I seen such a hopeless bloody washout!' He thought he heard a slight noise and stared around the tent, but it was empty. There was a sudden drumming on the canvas as the rain intensified. He held up his hand and, magically, it died away.

'Thank you, men. But you can't get round me as easily as that. I've heard all the excuses in the book from your Commanding Ossifer, General Pimm, but IT'S NOT GOOD ENOUGH! I'm going to spell it out. I'm going to turn my back on you . . .'

'Excuse me, sir.'

'Shut up, Pimm.'

60

'Right, sir.'

'I'm going to turn my back on you for ten minutes, and when I look round again I want to see this parade lined up in packets or boxes of the correct size, labels on straight, in apple-pie order FACING THE FRONT!'

His voice had risen to a scream. Suddenly he stopped. There had been a definite snort from somewhere on the right-hand side of the marquee and he thought he saw the table cloth tremble slightly. He was feeling a little dizzy, but was sure he hadn't imagined it. He leaped down from the platform to investigate. There was a sudden movement and a shriek from further along, and a whole section of the table collapsed with a crash. The cloth slid off sideways and began heaving and billowing as somebody fought to get out from under it. Suddenly it was flung off to reveal Amelia, sitting on the grass, groaning and spluttering at the same time, with a dish of trifle in her lap. Jerry stared at her in astonishment.

'What are you doing down there, Pimm?' he asked solemnly. She tried to comb salad out of her hair, beginning to giggle.

'I'm in an absolute mess.'

'Yes you are, Pimm. An officers' mess!' She collapsed in spurts of laughter, which Jerry joined in.

'Oh stop, stop . . . you're mad,' she gasped. 'Please, think of something sad. I can't stop.'

'I know,' he said, looking solemn. 'Begonias!'

She doubled up. 'They're . . . not . . . sad . . .'

'Well . . . school dinners then.'

'Yes!' she shrieked, trying to hold her mouth closed. 'Rice pudding!'

61

'Lost Property!'

'Single socks!'

'Double physics!'

'Navy-blue serge . . .'

'Knickers!' finished Jerry. He doubled up, too, and they both staggered around choking with laughter. Suddenly Amelia stopped and looked towards the entrance of the marquee. She put her hand on his own. The shock was about two thousand volts stronger this time.

'Did you hear anything?' she whispered. Jerry shook his head. They stared at each other in the gloomy green light. 'We shouldn't laugh . . . you shouldn't make fun of him like that.'

'I didn't mean . . . I was just messing about.'

She looked down. 'He wasn't always like this,' she said in a low voice. 'He used to be a terrific sport. He taught me to ride, you know. We used to go out every day . . . and he was terribly handsome.'

'Oh.' Jerry didn't know what to say. Amelia pressed her lips together. 'Yes. He's changed. Gran says it's called depression. But he seems to be angry all the time, and he's not supposed to get angry. The doctor told him it was bad for his health.' She suddenly laughed. 'He ought to have known that would only make him worse. He gets furious every time he remembers it! Talking of which, I'd better go. He'd go nuts if he knew I was with you.' She ran to the door, peered out, then looked back.

'By the way – I'm going riding this afternoon. I might look in on your den.'

Jerry was stunned. How did she know about that? 'OK,' he said, managing a shrug.

6 He soon figured out how Amelia knew about the island. She must have seen his rope hanging from the pine. He wondered if she'd discovered his 'cabin'. He decided to get there early so as to make everything ship-shape before she arrived, but he had to spend the rest of the morning getting his school stuff together.

By the time he reached the island the rain had stopped and hazy sunshine was breaking through the mist. Everything was dripping wet, growing almost visibly. Branches still showed like bare bones, but more were clothed in a cloud of buds. Bluebells hung like smoke in the clearing, and the beeches were out, in pale green feathery fronds. A woodpecker's tattoo rapped out, echoing among the trees. There was no sign of Amelia, but he searched the surrounding area thoroughly in case she was hiding. He didn't want to be taken by surprise again.

On the island, brambles and nettles were sprouting along the top of bank, screening his cabin even more. The dead briars were still in position, covering the hole. He pulled them away and lowered himself down. Everything was as he'd left it, the comics and ship's log (an old diary) unmoved. He concluded that she hadn't found it. He peered over the lip at the stream, swollen by the rains, rushing past only a few inches below. There was a shoal of tiny fish, darting and fanning like a shower of arrows. He stared at them for a while, hypnotised.

Then he climbed to his perch in the crown of the tree. He had brought an old pillowcase for a flag. He took it out and standing up, attached it to a branch as high up as he could reach. But there wasn't enough wind to make it fly, and it hung down limply, half hidden by the branches.

He settled back into the crow's-nest and looked across the tree-tops. Washes of misty rain broke over the wood. For the first time it occurred to him that she might not come. He closed his eyes and let the fine drops sprinkle his face. He could hear the faint chuckle of the stream far below, the slapping of the wet flag, the wind humming in the pine needles. Suddenly the name came to him. The *Windrush* he would call it, after the stream. He smelled the pine resin on his hands and felt the gentle sway of the tree, like a tall ship riding at anchor. It was good to be alone. He was now almost hoping that she wouldn't come. It had been good fun in the marquee, but he hadn't had time to feel self-conscious. He realised that he hardly knew her, and wondered what they would find to talk about. Then he remembered her grabbing his arm, and hoped she'd come anyhow. But there was no sight or sound of a horse and rider. The rain was falling more heavily now, collecting on his hair and trickling down his neck. It was past four. Maybe she'd been put off by the weather.

He thought of his old gang, the Quarry Raiders. They

were already fading into distant memories. He wondered about the new school. Everybody would have their mates, their places to sit in class and in the canteen, know the rules. He'd be the new boy, the outsider, starting in the third term of the year. The teachers would make nice remarks about looking after him and showing him the ropes, but it wouldn't make any difference. The others would be watching him, whispering to each other, or simply ignoring him completely. He shivered and pulled up the collar of his jacket. It was just something you had to get through. And he'd always had friends before . . . people liked you if you were funny.

Jerry shook the rain off his hair, like a dog. He knew she wasn't coming now. He felt disappointed. But after all, she'd only said she *might* come. And perhaps it was better. The *Windrush* was *his* ship. It was up to him to invite guests aboard, not up to them to invite themselves. She probably wouldn't have been able to climb the rope, anyway. Roly crept out from under a bush as Jerry jumped down.

'Do not despair, my old sea-dog!' he said. 'Never say die. We'll get this tub launched, by the Powers! Come with me.' He led Roly to the prow where a pointed rock cleaved the current. A twisted stump grew above it. From a certain angle this seemed to him to resemble a bird, a parrot in fact.

'Hmmm . . . the *Roaring Parrot* . . . I wonder if that's a better name, Roly.' The dog shook himself thoroughly, sending a shower of water over Jerry. 'No? You don't like that name. I see. Very well, the *Windrush* it shall be.'

Jerry took the bottle of Coca Cola out of his pocket, opened it and drank. 'No sense in wasting good liquor, my

65

old swab,' he said, standing to attention. 'I name this craft the good ship *Windrush*! May God bless her, and all who sail in her!'

Taking a last look round to make sure Amelia wasn't approaching, he hurled the bottle against the rocks. It bounced off and fell into the stream, which carried it swiftly out of sight.

'HIP HIP . . .' he yelled. Roly howled the 'HOOOORAAAY.' It was the saddest Hooray Jerry had ever heard. He ran home in the rain, hoping to sneak in unnoticed and change out of his wet clothes, but his mum and dad were already sitting down to supper and saw him come in.

'Are you trying to catch your death of cold, Jerry?' asked his mum.

'Good idea. I wouldn't have to start school if I was dead.'

'Well, at least he's not come in covered in mud with a couple of eggs in his mouth,' said his dad. 'We must be grateful for small mercies.' Jerry sat down in his underpants, picked up a knife like a dagger and stabbed a meat-ball.

'Haggis again,' he said gloomily.

'Now then, Jerry,' said his dad. 'The holiday's over and I'll be wanting a bit of help from you around the place.'

'What do you mean, Dad?'

'I'd like you to take responsibility for the chickens. It'll help your mother and me a lot.'

'How?'

'Easy. You let them out in the morning, before you go to school, feed them a saucepan of corn, there's a sack in the shed, make sure they've got water, and fetch in the eggs.

Then you close them up at night, last thing. Are you listening?'

Jerry had tilted his chair back on two legs. His head lolled sideways, eyes crossed, arms hanging limply by his sides.

'Yes, Dad.' It was the voice of a zombie.

'Well, be sure you do. They're Captain Packham's hens, don't forget, not ours. So we don't want anything happening to them.'

'No, Dad.' He brought his chair down with a crash. 'Hey! Why do we have to look after them, if they're his hens?'

'Part of the job, son, and there it is. We're allowed to keep a dozen eggs a week.'

'That's not many,' said Jerry. His mum and dad exchanged a glance.

'And once a week, you muck them out and give them fresh straw. Wilf'll show you where it is. You can do that on Saturday mornings, *before* you get your pocket money.'

Jerry smiled grimly. 'I get the picture . . . no muck no money, huh?'

'Well, they do say "wheres there's muck there's brass".' laughed his dad.

'Do they? I've never heard anyone say that.'

'You've not heard everything, you know, sunshine.'

Jerry cocked his head. A car was approaching down the drive from the direction of Battlefields. He raced to the front room and looked out of the window. It was a red Volvo Estate. The driver was a man he hadn't seen before. Amelia was sitting in the front passenger seat. As the car swept past, their eyes met. She pulled a wry face and shrugged. He just had time to raise his hand in a wave. The car stopped briefly at the junction before turning into the lane. Jerry could see Amelia's head through the big rear window. She didn't turn round.

The first chance he got, Jerry asked Wilf when Amelia would be coming back.

'She won't,' he said, leaning on his spade and puffing a bit. 'Leastways not till summer, unless she comes at half-term. I won't say that's impossible.'

Jerry was shocked. Because Amelia had been at Battlefields ever since he'd moved in, he'd come to think of her as living there. 'Well, where's she gone?' he asked. 'She's not going back to school for another week. She told me.'

'That's right. She's off to Austria or Switzerland or one of them places, winter-sporting.'

This made it even worse. 'Do you know the name of her school?' Wilf looked at Jerry with a twinkle in his eye.

'Didn't she tell you?' Jerry looked embarrassed. 'Lord no,' went on Wilf. 'I ain't got a notion . . . saving it's up in Lincolnshire, I believe. I could perhaps find it out for you.'

'No . . . don't bother . . . it doesn't matter.' He knew he'd never have the nerve to write.

'How was it, your first day?'

'Oh . . . all right. They don't do drama though.'

'What's that?'

'You know, acting . . . making up plays . . . it's my best subject.'

Wilf chuckled. 'I reckon it would be . . . I tell you what though, seems to me we're all doing that anyhow . . . sort of making up the parts as we go along like.'

Jerry frowned. 'What do you mean?'

68

'I dunno. I'm probably going crackers in my old age. Did you find out about the battle yet?'

'I haven't had a chance . . . I'll ask in history.'

'Go and have a look in the church,' said Wilf. 'You'll find summat interesting in there.'

'We're not allowed into the town,' he replied. 'But I'll be going in with Mum, I expect.'

In fact, school wasn't half as bad as he'd expected. He'd been put next to a boy called Nat, who'd fallen out with his best friend Greg in the holidays. Nat was burly and rather bossy, but he'd taken a fancy to Jerry. He kept asking him questions about Coventry and said he was going to live there as soon as he left school. Jerry perfected an impersonation of Mr Robinson, the Maths teacher, saying 'Come along now, kiddies,' which made Nat laugh so much he fell off his chair.

He soon got into the routine: up at 7.00, let chickens out, breakfast, cycle to Ducklington, coach to school, work, work, work, coach to Ducklington, cycle home, tea, homework, chores, TV, chickens, bed. Roly was always peering out of the front window eagerly to welcome him home and Jerry would stand like a statue in the hall while the dog leapt up, butted his cap off with his paws and then shook it like a rat. Roly had a thing about hats. He couldn't stand them.

The other useful thing Roly did about the house was to fetch the newspaper and mail to Jerry at breakfast time. If there wasn't any mail, he'd bring the telephone directory instead. Of course the mail was hardly ever for Jerry, so he just thanked Roly very solemnly and put it on the table for his parents. But on the second Saturday of term Roly came

69

in panting importantly, carrying a postcard. Jerry saw some snow gleaming on the picture (it had got rather wet) and snatched it out of his mouth. Suddenly he knew it was from Amelia. It was split into four scenes: a chair-lift slung from cables, a village half buried in snow; a red sunset over snowy mountains and a café with some jolly-looking people on the terrace. On the back was his name and address in a neat round handwriting. But the message was in French!

'Il fait beau ici tous les jours. La neige est belle. Dommage que je n'ai pas vu ton terrier dans le bois, mais j'etais interdit par mon grand-père.' It was signed *'Pim'*.

He grinned.

'May I see?' asked Mrs Mills. He handed it to her. She frowned. 'But it's foreign . . . who is Pim?'

'Oh, my contact over there,' he said mysteriously. 'That's only his codename of course.' Mrs Mills sighed.

'I should have known better than to expect a straight answer, I suppose.'

'It's just that I'm not at liberty to discuss certain matters, Mum, even with intimate members of my family. Official Secrets and all that sort of thing. You'll just have to trust me, I'm afraid. The security of the free world hangs in the balance.'

He rushed off to his room to consult the French dictionary. Half an hour later his hair was sticking up in strange tufts and spikes and he had a page covered with scribbles and crossings-out. As far as he could make out, it said, 'It makes nice here all the days. The snow is beautiful. Shame that I have not seen your terrier in the wood, but I have been forbidden by my grandfather.'

So that was why she hadn't turned up. But surely she

70

didn't think Roly was a terrier? He was puzzled about this until he checked the dictionary again and found that another meaning of the word 'terrier' was den or earth. He decided to reply. Then he realised she hadn't given her school address. He wondered how he could get hold of it. Wilf didn't know it and he didn't really want to ask him to find out. There was no question of asking Captain Packham. On the few occasions Jerry had seen him being driven past the Gatehouse he had stared straight in front with a sour expression, totally ignoring him. But what about Mrs Packham? She might give him the address. Still he hesitated. But he was only replying to Amelia's card.

A couple of weeks later he got his chance. Jerry had a day off school because his teachers were doing a training course. Wilf asked him to take a currycomb up to Mrs Packham. Jerry hadn't been to Battlefields since the Sunday he'd met Amelia in the marquee and everything looked different. The daffodils were over, but the neat flower beds were bright with tulips, pansies and wallflowers. Jerry felt proud of his dad's work. He went to the courtyard and looked nervously round. All was quiet. He rang the bell. Mrs Packham answered the door and he breathed a sigh of relief.

'Oh! Hello, Jamie,' she exclaimed. 'How nice of you to call.' It was too late to correct this error. He was doomed always to be Jamie to Mrs Packham.

'Hello, Mrs Packham. I brought this.' He handed her the comb. 'Wilf said to give it to you.'

'Oh. Thank you so much. You have to groom them every day, you know, otherwise they get out of . . .'

'I just wondered . . . could I have Amelia's address

71

please? She . . . sent me a postcard, you see, and I wanted to reply.'

'Amelia's address! You mean her school address?'

'Yes.'

'Why certainly . . . a postcard . . . did she?'

'From Austria.'

'Yes . . . she had a wonderful . . . now, let me think . . . Come in a minute, Jamie . . .'

She went over to the dresser and picked up a note-pad. 'I'll jot it down for you . . . It's St. Patrick's, of course . . .' She wrote something down, tore off the sheet and looked at Jerry with an odd expression.

'Here you are . . . you won't . . . um . . . mention this, will you?' she said, handing it to him. He glanced at the address: St. Patrick's School, Huntley, Lincolnshire. Mrs Packham lit a cigarette and drew deeply on it. 'You see . . . Leonard wouldn't understand at all,' she said, more definitely than usual. 'He's rather old-fashioned . . . actually he still thinks of Amelia as quite a little girl . . .'

'Thanks,' said Jerry. 'I won't.' He turned to go but Mrs Packham carried on.

'Perhaps not old-fashioned . . . Leonard doesn't like the way things have changed. He's a great patriot . . . I suppose *that's* unfashionable now . . . but he loves this country. It's what he fought for, and he was a fine soldier, you know. But it was the Old England that he fought for, as it used to be when we were young, and it's changed so much . . . so very much . . . you can't imagine. He just doesn't feel as if he belongs in it any more . . . do you understand? . . . As if he's been left high and dry on the beach . . . obsolete.' She gave a sudden harsh laugh. 'Like an old man-o'-war!'

72

A door slammed somewhere in the house. Mrs Packham jumped and dropped the box of matches she was holding. Jerry went to pick them up, but she ushered him to the door. 'So perhaps this had better be our little secret . . .' she said.

Jerry nodded. 'Don't worry . . . and thanks, Mrs Packham . . .'

Outside in the courtyard, he paused. If that had been the front door slamming it meant that Captain Packham was outside somewhere. He decided to cut back through the fields so as to make sure of avoiding him, but as he crossed the cobbles there was a sudden crashing noise and a grating howl from the stables. Brutus must have heard him or caught his scent. The door shook violently as he hurled himself repeatedly against it. A shout came from the direction of the rose garden. In desperation Jerry dived into one of the out-buildings that was used as a garage and crouched down behind the car.

Sticks rapped over the cobblestones now and Packham's voice rang out.

'Shut up! Shut up! Damn you!' Jerry froze, hardly daring to breathe. There was a bang as one of the crutches hit the door, and the crashing and howling ceased, replaced by a miserable whining. He could hear Packham's laboured breathing in the silence that followed. Suddenly he shouted again.

'Mills! COME HERE!' For an instant Jerry thought he was discovered and half rose. Then he heard footsteps and realised that Packham was addressing his father. He ducked down again.

'Have you been up here, Mills?'

'Well . . . not recently, sir.'

'Are you sure about that?'

'Yes, sir . . . I was up here about . . .'

'Never mind. Never mind. What about that hedge?'

'I was just going off for my dinner, sir.'

'I see . . . you mean lunch, I suppose. Well – it's not satisfactory. I can't have you sloping off like this all the time . . .'

'But . . . I've always gone home for dinner, sir.'

'I dare say. Not any more. Not my people.'

'But, sir . . .'

'Don't argue with me, Mills, dammit. I won't have it. From now on, sandwiches, d'you see?'

There was a silence.

'Well, I'm expected back for dinner today, sir, so . . .'

'No back-chat, Mills,' snapped Packham. 'Don't push your luck. Jobs don't grow on trees . . . especially at your time of life, eh? Is that why you lost your last job . . . back-chat?'

'No, sir. I was made redundant.'

'Redundant!' Packham laughed nastily. 'We all know what that means. Just a fancy word for . . .'

Jerry jammed his fists over his ears. He couldn't bear to hear any more. The bleating voice and tapping sticks passed out of the courtyard. For a long time he just crouched in the corner of the garage, as silent and still as the car. Finally he sneaked out without being seen and ran home through the fields. His parents had finished dinner and there was a tense feeling in the house, as if they'd been having a row.

'Where on earth have you been, Jerry?' asked his mum crossly.

'Out for a walk.'

74

'Out where? Your food's dried up by now, I should think.' Jerry silently sat down to his food.

'Well, answer your mother,' said his dad. 'Out where?'

'Just out.'

'You get back here on time for meals in future.' Jerry didn't answer.

'All right?' persisted his father.

'ALL RIGHT!'

His father raised his hand to strike Jerry, but restrained himself, and smashed it down on the table instead. 'You keep a civil tongue in your head,' he shouted.

Jerry pushed his plate aside. 'I'm not hungry anyway.'

'You damned well eat it up, my lad. Your mother's taken the trouble to cook it.'

'Now then, Victor!' said his mum. 'If he's . . .'

'No!' His dad stood up. 'I'm not having him pandered to, like some wet . . .'

Jerry had got up too. A wave of anger swept over him.

'You're the wet!' he yelled, and ran out of the room.

He lay on his bed and listened to his parents shouting at each other. Eventually he heard the front door slam and footsteps on the stairs. There was a tap on his door. His mum came in. 'You're to stay in your room for the rest of the day,' she said. 'How could you speak to your father like that?'

He burst into tears. She sat down on the bed and put her arm round him.

'Things aren't easy at the moment. I want you to make peace with your father, and never speak like that again. Whatever made you say it?'

Jerry was sobbing so hard he couldn't speak. Finally he

75

managed to stammer out. 'I h . . . heard them.' His mother stiffened and her grip tightened on his shoulder.

'Heard who?' she asked sharply.

'Them . . . Dad and Captain Packham . . . He spoke to Dad like he was . . . dirt . . . and Dad didn't . . . didn't . . .'

'I know,' she interrupted. 'I know. And I'll tell you why he didn't answer back. For your sake and mine. He's more of a man for it.'

Jerry sat up. 'No, Mum. He's not. A man would have smashed him in the face for saying that.'

'What? Hit an old man on crutches? Where's the bravery in that?'

'He deserves it. I would have.'

'Would you, Jerry? And what would be the result if he had? Your dad loses his job and probably gets taken to court. We have to pack up and move when we've only just settled in. We're back on the dole and no reference to help find another job.' Jerry was silent.

'Maybe I wouldn't hit him . . . but . . . I wouldn't work for someone like that . . . I'd just leave.'

His mum sighed. 'You don't understand, Jerry. You haven't got responsibilities.'

'Doesn't he care if everyone hates him?'

'Look, Jerry – he's afraid. People don't care what anyone thinks when they're afraid.'

'Afraid? Afraid of what?'

'Old age . . . pain . . . going to sleep and not waking up next day . . . being crippled – dependent on people. Remember, he was an active man. A bit of a hero in his time. Now what's he got?'

'More than us.'

'No. That he hasn't!' she said angrily. 'You think what you're saying – think how lucky, how very lucky you are – your whole life before you, not behind you.'

Jerry stared out of the window. 'But it's not fair . . . not letting Dad come home for lunch.'

'I know,' said Mrs Mills. 'But it's not a case of what's fair. It's like it or lump it. There's no Union of Gardeners . . . and even if there was, and Vic complained to it, he'd only lose the job.'

'Tell Dad I'm sorry then,' said Jerry at last.

'I will – but you must apologise to him yourself. He's very upset. He says you're to stay in your room for the rest of the day.'

Jerry nodded. 'I don't mind,' he said. 'I wasn't going anywhere.'

'I'll bring your tea up later,' she said as she went out.

Jerry tried to write a homework essay that was overdue, but his mind kept wandering back to the conversation he'd overheard. Packham had spoken like some teachers did. He didn't think that happened when you grew up. And how was it manly to put up with it? That wasn't what heroes did in books or films. If somebody insulted them, they fought it out . . . or shot it out. Of course, he knew things weren't like that in the real world, but surely you didn't just put up with *any* insult or humiliation? Surely you had to draw the line somewhere. He didn't like to think of his dad being spoken to like that. It chewed him up inside.

During the long evening he gazed out of his window at the deepening dark, going over it again and again in his mind. The familiar outline of shed, trees and telegraph poles melted into gloom. Even when he finally went to bed he couldn't get it off his mind. Yes, it all belonged to Packham. He might be old and frightened but he still owned everything and told everybody what to do. And it was owning everything that gave him that power. Everything was his. The house, the garden, the trees, the chickens . . . suddenly he remembered. He hadn't shut away the chickens for the night.

'Let him put his own damned chickens away,' he thought. 'Anyway, I'm not allowed to leave my room.' And with this gesture of defiance he was at last able to sleep.

He was woken early by the cackling of the hens. It was barely light. He had been in the middle of an odd vivid dream. He was standing with a small group of people on a grassy plain. They were all flying kites. The strong wind was blowing huge white clouds rapidly across the sky and making waves in the grass. The kites were all silk and shaped like birds, each one different. They tossed and dived in the wind, but one was still, as if nailed to the sky. Jerry saw that it was a large hawk, flown by Captain Packham, who was standing a little apart from the group.

'See that kite of his,' somebody whispered. Jerry turned. It was Wilf, pointing up at Packham's kite. 'That'll keep all the small game skulking in the grass. All them partridges and pheasants and rabbits, once they feel the shadow on 'em they stay still, see, till he's close enough. Then he beats 'em out and shoots 'em.' With a start Jerry realised that what he had taken for a crutch under Packham's arm, was in fact a gun.

Jerry looked at his own kite. It was a tiny fluttering lark, high above the others, hovering like Packham's, but, unlike his, singing gaily.

'Look! Mine's the highest,' he cried. Packham heard and turned on him, his face twisted in a false grin.

'We'll see about that,' he shouted. 'Watch out for the hawk!' He paid out the string so that the hawk rose higher and higher, but when still below the lark it stopped. Packham had come to the end of the reel. He cursed, took out some huge old-fashioned shears from his jacket, and cut his own kite string with them. The hawk, suddenly released, soared up above the lark and then, running out of wind, swooped towards it. At the last minute Jerry tugged his string. The lark jinked sideways and the hawk missed its mark. He turned to Packham. He had collapsed like a puppet whose strings have been cut, and was lying in a crumpled heap on the ground. One of his arms was bent the wrong way at the elbow. Jerry looked round for Wilf, but everyone had disappeared. They were alone. He bent over Packham. His eyes were closed and he was very pale. Then Jerry saw something moving out of the corner of his eye. It was a small round bowl revolving slowly on the ground. He stared at it, hypnotised. It was filling with some dark liquid. The shocking realisation that this might be blood had woken him up.

He lay in bed thinking about the dream, and listening to the cackling hens. Slowly he became aware that the sound was unusual: a short squawk followed by a long one, repeated over and over again, like an alarm siren. Then there was a wild flapping of wings and a peculiar thumping noise, as if a heavy object were being dashed against the ground. He leapt out of bed and looked out of the window. In the dim light he could see a chicken flapping around in the pen. There was something clumsy about its movements. Then he realised: it didn't have a head. It flopped over and lay on the ground twitching. A long shape flickered through the shadows and pounced on another hen. A fox was in the run!

7 Jerry dashed downstairs in his pyjamas, through the kitchen and out into the garden, followed by Roly barking excitedly. The fox's head snicked round at the noise. It dropped the hen it was holding in its jaws and ran to the wire. Jerry burst through the gate, yelling madly. The fox stopped by the wire, turned for a second and looked straight at him. It was a beautiful young dog-fox, russet-red and black, with a white tip on its bushy tail. Roly went for it, barking furiously. But before he reached it the fox ran up the wire, scrambled over the top, leaped into the long grass and disappeared through a hedge. Roly seemed to go wild. He threw himself at the wire a couple of times, then began to race round the pen, making the hens even more hysterical. Jerry stared round in dismay. He could see four bodies, lying in puffs of brown and white feathers. He knew he was going to get the blame for this.

The back door slammed and his father came rushing out.

'What is it, Jerry?' he cried. 'What the devil's going on?' Then he saw the bodies and stopped.

'Bloody hell-fire! What's that dog done now?'

Jerry stared at his dad, not understanding the words. He looked at Roly, now running from one dead hen to the next. There was blood on his muzzle. In a flash of horror, he saw what his father was thinking.

'No! Not Roly! Not Roly, Dad. It was a fox!'

'Fox? There's no fox here.'

'It's gone . . . it went over the wire . . . I saw it.' His father looked at him steadily.

'I don't know, Jerry . . . this is a bad day's work . . . Very bad. How many's dead?'

'Four, I think.' Jerry managed to grab Roly's collar and tried to calm him down while his dad looked under the chicken-house. He emerged, looking dazed.

'There's another one in there scared half to death . . . looks like its blinded.' He stared at Roly. 'Are you sure it was a fox, Jerry?'

'Of course, Dad. I told you. I saw it go over the wire.'

'I've never heard of a fox going over a wire. That's why they put wire there – to keep them out.'

'Well IT DID,' shouted Jerry. His father turned on him angrily.

'And whose job was it to shut them up at night, so this couldn't happen?'

For a moment Jerry didn't know what to say. Then he remembered. 'You told me to stay in my room!'

His dad looked so taken aback that Jerry felt sorry for him. 'I don't know. There's four dead, maybe five, and the rest so frightened they'll probably not lay for weeks. I'm the one that's got to carry the can. It'll be docked off my wages and that won't be the end of it!'

'I'm sorry, Dad.'

82

'Sorry isn't good enough. Sorry won't bring them back to life, will it?'

Jerry's mum had come up in her dressing gown.

'It could be worse,' she said. 'If he hadn't come down they might all be dead. Why don't we just replace them and say nothing about it. They'd never know.'

Jerry's dad frowned. 'Because we can't. That's not my way, Cath.'

'But, Vic, if he was a reasonable man it'd be different . . .'

'That's not the point. These things always come out, and then how would we feel? I have got some pride left. I was brought up to tell the truth. I always have, and I'm not stopping now!' He walked angrily into the house. Jerry's mum looked at him, her mouth set in a thin line.

'There'll be trouble, I just know there will. Did you do it on purpose, Jerry?'

He hesitated. 'I don't know . . . I suppose so. But I didn't mean this to happen.'

'You might have known . . .'

'But, one night, Mum. I don't know the fox would come on the one night I didn't shut them up.'

'I expect it comes every night.'

'But why did it kill so many . . . it couldn't eat all these?'

'I've heard that they'll kill every chicken in the house, and leave them. They just go mad.'

'I didn't know,' he repeated, shaking his head.'

'Well, what's done is done, and we must take the consequences. I'm afraid you've lost your pocket money for a good few weeks.'

But that wasn't the worst of it. That night at supper his

83

parents were usually silent. Jerry suddenly felt that something dreadful was going to happen.

'Well . . . what did he say? What's happened now?' he asked. His dad put down his knife and fork and glanced at his mum.

'We've got some bad news I'm afraid, Jerry. Roley's got to go.'

Jerry stared at him, not taking it in. His mum got up and left the room.

'Go? Go where?'

'What I mean to say is that he can't stay here with us . . .' Jerry stood up, eyes fixed on his dad in horror.

'Now calm down . . . take it easy . . .'

'DAD!'

'Look, Packham blew his top about the chickens . . . he's got it into his head that Roly did it . . .'

'Why should he think that? You didn't tell him that, did you?'

'Of course not, Jerry. But you know what he's like. He wouldn't listen. Came ranting and raving down here to see for himself. "There's no hole in the wire," he says. "It couldn't be a fox." I told him what you saw. "That boy's a liar," he says, "he's covering up for the dog".'

'No!' Jerry's mind reeled. He felt sick with rage. 'I'm not a liar. I saw it. Didn't you tell him?'

'I keep telling you, he wouldn't listen. He said Roly was vicious . . . attacked him at the garden party.'

'DAD! It's a lie. You know that. You should have stood up to him.'

His dad was on his feet now, facing Jerry across the table. 'That's right, blame me!' he shouted. 'It's a hard world out

84

there, Jerry – you'll find out one day!'

'You didn't stand up to him!' shouted Jerry again. 'You're a coward . . . I hate you for this! I hate you!'

'Don't speak to me like that!' •

'He's MINE,' yelled Jerry. 'He's not yours! He's not Packham's! He's MINE and I'm keeping him!'

'STOP THIS!' His mum had come back in, wiping her eyes. 'Listen to me, Jerry,' she went on in a trembling voice. 'We've called John. He's agreed to look after Roly for the time being.'

'NO!'

Jerry grabbed Roly's collar and tugged him out of the room and upstairs to his bedroom. He barricaded the door by dragging a chest of drawers across it and ignored his mother's pleas to open it. When she'd gone he sat on the floor for ages fondling Roly and comforting him, telling him repeatedly that he wouldn't be sent away. Suddenly he sat up and took a crumpled bit of paper out of his pocket. On it was written 'St. Patrick's School, Huntley in Lincolnshire'. He got out some writing paper and started writing:

'Dear Amelia, Thanks for your card. It was nice to hear from you. Well, I've got a *real* problem. Roly is being blamed for killing some chickens, but he didn't. I know because I saw the fox. Roly wouldn't do anything like that, as you know. But your grandad wants to send him away. I'm wondering if you could do anything to help – I know its a cheek to ask but I'm *DESPERATE*. Maybe you could ask your grandad to give him another chance? Don't worry if you can't, just say and I'll understand. Thanks. Jerry.'

Next day was Wednesday. He wrote 'URGENT' all over

the envelope and posted the letter in Ducklington. His mum told him that his older brother John was coming down from Coventry at the weekend. So that only gave Amelia two days, or three at the most, if she got the letter on Thursday. He tried to imagine her relationship with Packham. Did she have any influence over him? The way he'd spoken to her in the car-park didn't give him much hope. And the days went by without any reprieve from Battlefields. On Thursday Roly brought in a couple of brown envelopes for Jerry's dad. On Friday he brought in the Yellow Pages, because there wasn't any mail. Jerry began to despair. Amelia couldn't do anything against someone like Packham, even if he was her grandfather. And why should she put herself out for Jerry anyway? They hardly knew each other. He regretted that he'd written to her now. But she was still his only hope. He couldn't concentrate on the lessons at school, and got a lunch-time detention. His friend Nat couldn't get any jokes or funny voices out of him, and dropped him for his previous friend Greg.

Saturday came, a grey clammy morning with mist in the air. There was no letter, or message from Battlefields. Jerry hadn't spoken to his dad since their row on Tuesday night. His mum told him that John was coming in the afternoon and staying the night. He would set off with Roly first thing on Sunday morning. She tried to cheer him up at breakfast.

'You never know,' she said. 'Captain Packham may change his mind – then we could have Roly back again. It'll help us out for John to have him for a while. He's quite an expense, you know.'

Jerry didn't answer. There was an ache in his throat that wouldn't go away. So Amelia had let him down. He'd been stupid to think she would help. She was one of them. Why should she help him? Jerry began to collect Roly's things together for him to take: the heavy wooden skittle ball that he played football with, Jerry's old school cap chewed to an unrecognisable rag, the emu and the panda with only one ear. His current favourite was the emu. He kept trying to bat it out of Jerry's hands, for a game. It was obvious that he didn't understand what was going to happen. For all his intelligence, this was the limit of his understanding. For the first time there was a barrier between them. Jerry realised that he could not communicate about the past or the future with Roly. He could only share the present moment with him. Then an even worse thought struck him. Roly might think Jerry had sent him away. He rolled on his bed in anguish at this idea. Roly tried to lick away his tears.

Jerry didn't go downstairs for lunch. He heard his brother's car arrive and a while later there was a knock on the bedroom door. John put his head in.

'Hello, Jerry. Can I come in?' Jerry nodded. John came up and put his hand on Jerry's shoulder. 'How goes it?' he said kindly. Jerry burst into tears.

'I know. I know. It's hard. And I'm right sorry to be the one that takes him away, I can tell you. But it's better me than a stranger. I know what he means to you.'

'You don't,' cried Jerry. 'Nobody does. I've got to have him. He's my only . . .' He was going to say 'friend' but was overcome with sobbing. His brother sat down on the bed.

'Listen, Jerry . . . it's just for the time being. I know he's yours. I'm looking after him for *you*. We'll find a way round this, you see. You won't be here for ever. Even if Dad stayed on, you could come up to Coventry when you leave school . . .' Jerry rubbed his arm across his eyes.

'Oh yes . . . three years!' It sounded like for ever. Twenty-one dog years.

'It'll pass in no time and you could stop with me and go to the Tech. You're bright enough to do what you like, you know. Just make up your mind to work hard and get all the qualifications you can. That's the way out of this.' He glanced towards the door. 'Our dad never had the chance, you know. His father died when he was only a kid. He had to go out to work to support his mother. But you can do anything, pick and choose, go anywhere. You've got the brains.'

Jerry shook his head. 'He won't understand. He won't know why he's being sent away.'

John sighed. 'I'll take good care of him. What's his favourite? Does he still like cucumber?' Jerry nodded.

'There you are – I remembered. I'll feed him up. Nothing but the best.'

'I'm taking him for a walk,' said Jerry, getting up. 'I'll see you later.'

They went aboard the *Windrush*. Jerry had rigged up a gangplank so you could walk across to the island. He pulled it up after him once they were over, like a draw-bridge, to prevent anyone following. He didn't climb the mast, but sat in the cabin with Roly, staring into the glassy water. He felt numb. It was impossible to imagine life without Roly. But, in a way, it felt as if he'd already gone. He scrutinised every detail of the dog, from the black spot on his ear to his stumpy tail, determined that he wouldn't forget what he looked like. Finally he fell asleep. It was dusk when he woke up. He walked slowly back to the Gatehouse, so that it was quite dark by the time he reached it. At the back door he hesitated. Wilf's kitchen light was on, and his door ajar. Jerry hadn't seen him about since the trouble started. On an impulse, he tapped on the door, and when there was no reply, pushed it open and looked in. Wilf was sprawled back in his wooden armchair with his eyes closed. A bottle and glass were on the table. He opened his eyes, rubbed his face and stared uncomprehendingly at Jerry, then suddenly recognised him.

'Come on in, lad,' he cried. 'How are ye doing?' He poured himself a drink of some golden liquid. His face was very red and his voice thick.

'OK,' said Jerry. 'Well . . . not too good. My brother's come to fetch Roly. He's . . .'

'I know, I know,' interrupted Wilf. 'Take a seat.' He waved towards a chair and Jerry sat down.

'It wasn't Roly that killed the chickens . . .' he began.

'I know that!' said Wilf again. 'And so does Packham, never fear . . .'

Jerry looked up. 'Does he?'

'Ay! 'Course he does. But he don't care . . . he wants to get rid of it, and that's that.' He drained his glass and poured another. 'Oh! It ain't right,' he added, seeing the anguish in Jerry's face. 'Old story . . . Did you look in the church, like I said?'

'I haven't had a chance yet,' said Jerry, rising to go.

'No . . . wait!' said Wilf urgently. 'Wait a second. I want to tell you summat.'

Jerry reluctantly sat down again. He hadn't seen Wilf like this before.

'In that church,' he continued, 'you'll see my name . . . Sedley . . . and it's not on a tombstone neither. It were scratched on the lead font with the point of a dagger. "Antony Sedley" and then the word "PRISNER 1649".'

'But . . . your name's Wilf not Antony.'

Wilf snorted. 'Pay attention! That weren't me. This were in 1649 – more'n 300 years ago. I may be old, but I ain't that old!' He chuckled and drained his glass. 'No! This were more'n likely an ancestor of mine, as I do believe, kept a prisoner in the church. Want to know why?' Jerry was interested in spite of everything. He nodded. Wilf stared into space.

'Well, it were to do with that battle that took place hereabouts. Battle of Burford. Only it weren't much of a battle. I was born and bred in these parts but nobody knows owt about it round here, or anywhere else that I can see. I only digged down into it because of the feller in the church having my name like.' Jerry shifted impatiently.

'Jus' listen!' insisted Wilf. 'I ain't tellin' you this for fun! Well, 1649 were slap bang in the middle of the Civil Wars. It were in January that year they cut off King Charlie's head, if you know your history. They had a chance then . . . a chance to make a clean start. There was a bunch called The Levellers . . . all for equality . . . said "Why should one man have a thousand acres and a thousand have nowt? Let's level it up" they said . . . "take it away from him . . . split it up among the others, all fair and square . . . so everyone's got a bit of property to call their own . . ." Silly idea!'

'Why? What's silly about it?'

Wilf leaned forward. 'Well, have you noticed folk giving

90

away their property? Not likely! They hang on to it.' He clawed the edge of the table to demonstrate. 'Like grim death! And the more they've got, the tighter they hang on!' Jerry noticed the veins standing out wrinkling the tattoos on his muscular arms.

'Were they Roundheads or Cavaliers?' he asked.

'Roundheads, of course! They weren't for the King . . . he was the biggest landowner of the lot! No, they were all for Cromwell, and he was all for them. Got 'em into his army fighting for him, he did. Told 'em they was going to have a proper democratic system like, with votes for everyone, not just the landowners. And they fought for him too – The New Model Army they called it. They even elected the officers!' Wilf laughed. 'Yes. They fought and won. Cromwell got in. What d'you think he did then?'

Jerry shrugged.

'You can guess, can't you? Helped himself to a big estate out of the King's lands . . . handed out some to his cronies, and forgot all about LEVELLING!' There was a bitterness in Wilf's face which Jerry hadn't noticed before. Wilf leaned forward again and spoke softly now.

'But these Levellers, they wouldn't give up, see. They knew they was right. So they kept on going, printing pamphlets, getting supporters . . . turned out a lot of people agreed with them. Cromwell get's worried . . . he's had a taste of power and he likes it. "If this idea catches on," he says to himself, "what'll happen to me and my mates? We'll be knocked back down to one acre again. Best nip this in the bud," he says. . . . he's the King himself now, see. Calls himself "Protector"! Dictator's more the mark! Says them as don't agree with him is traitors . . .'

91

'Traitors!' exclaimed Jerry.

'Ay! Scarce believe it, would you? There was only one traitor and that were him. But he gets his bully-boys and attacks these Levellers as they was camped out for the night in that field over there. A lot of them was religious men. Do you know what day of the week it was?'

'No.'

'Sunday! Ay – he broke all the rules. They had rules for fighting in them days, but Cromwell broke 'em all. Took 'em by surprise, by night, on a Sunday . . . Poor sods, they didn't know what hit 'em . . . a lot ran . . . he takes three hundred and some prisoners and locks 'em up in the church. My ancestor, Antony Sedley, were one of 'em. Cromwell tells 'em he's going to shoot the lot, lets 'em think about that a couple of days, then he shoots three of 'em right in front of the others. That were enough. That cured it. British bloody revolution! Three bullets. See what I mean?' He stared at Jerry with a puzzled angry expression.

Jerry struggled to understand. 'I only know it's not fair,' he said at last.

'But that's just it!' cried Wilf. 'There's no such thing as fair. Not when you're up against somebody as holds all the cards.'

Jerry sighed. 'I don't get it,' he said.

'No,' said Wilf. 'Neither do I really. What I'm trying to tell you is it's all happened before. Nothing's changed much . . . I haven't got any answers . . . it's just the same . . . same old ground . . . same old battle . . .'

His eyes were beginning to fade. He was looking at Jerry as if he were very far away. Suddenly his head slumped forward on to his arms and he began snoring loudly.

Jerry got up as quietly as he could and tip-toed out.

Jerry woke the next morning with a feeling of dread. He lay in bed thinking about how it always came, as you knew it would, the day when something bad was going to happen: the appointment with the dentist, or the examination, or the bully picking a fight, or the teacher making you stand in front of the class to do something you couldn't do. And when it came, everything slowed down and waited to see what you'd do.

Jerry didn't get up or respond when they came into his bedroom to take Roly. He lay facing the wall, hating them for it. But when he heard the engine start, he dashed to the landing window. It was raining. Through the streaked pane he saw the car pull away. Suddenly Roly's white face appeared at the back window. He didn't see Jerry. He was barking, but it sounded very faint and far away, as if he were on the other end of a telephone line. The car disappeared round the corner. The barking faded until it was only an echo in Jerry's mind.

The house seemed cheerless without him, like a cold room without a fire. The spirit had gone out of it, not just because of Roly's absence, but because of the defeat and humiliation which it represented.

Jerry was resentful, his dad was silent. They avoided each other, sensing that any conversation would quickly turn into a row. His mum was not happy either. He would often see her staring out of the window, her eyes full of sadness.

One time he heard her crying in her room when she thought he was out. He wanted to comfort her, but had nothing to give. He must have made a slight noise on the landing, because she stopped suddenly and opened the door before he had time to go.

'Jerry!'

'Don't worry, Mum,' he said feebly.

'I can't help it.' She sank down on to the bed. 'I think we've made a mistake coming here. We ought to have known.'

Jerry put his arm round her. 'Can't we just go?'

'It's not as simple as that. Go where? We're not even on the waiting list for a council place; and we've got no savings. Packham doesn't pay enough to save on.'

Jerry thought about this.

'Have things changed much?' he asked suddenly.

'What do you mean?'

'I mean . . . since the old days . . . since Cromwell . . . Wilf said . . .'

''Course they've changed.' She blew her nose and went over to the mirror. 'Everything's changed. Look at medicine. Kids used to be sick all the time. A lot died. And conveniences. My mother used to spend a whole day a week just washing . . . and ironing every night. And if you fell ill, you'd likely lose your job, and if you did, there wasn't any dole . . .' She looked at Jerry in the mirror. 'Yes, things have changed all right. It's just that some people don't seem

95

to realise it.'

'I'm not going to rent a house when I grow up,' said Jerry after a while. 'I'm going to own one. Then nobody can tell me what to do.'

'I hope you will,' said his mum.

'And you can come and live in it with me . . . You and Dad.'

She suddenly hugged him and burst into tears again.

He never went by the track from Dead Pine Corner these days. Part of it was visible from Battlefields and he would get a prickly feeling in the middle of his back, as if Packham were watching him through binoculars, or the sights of a powerful rifle. His idea of the countryside had changed. It was no longer a wilderness full of secret places to explore. The unseen power of Packham hovered over the fields like a bird of prey, casting a shadow even on the public footpaths and rights of way.

Spring turned into summer. The pale fresh colours faded into a uniform dark green, often with overcast grey skies above. The still hot woods seemed dull, choked with nettles and brambles. Things didn't go well at school either. Nat had taken a peculiar dislike to him and persecuted him at every opportunity. He acquired a reputation for being sullen with the teachers, who began to see him as a misfit. There weren't any boys his age in the area, so he spent his spare time alone, reading or watching TV, or just gazing out of his bedroom window, head on his arms, day-dreaming.

Packham was off his crutches and Jerry often saw him driving past in his black BMW. He never stopped at the corner to see if anything was coming down the lane. John rang regularly, once a week, to report on Roly. The third time he rang he sounded rather cross.

'I don't know what's the matter with him,' he said. 'He keeps chewing up my carpets. And wetting in the house. He's never done that before, has he?'

'No! Not since he was a pup.'

'And another thing. He can't settle down unless he can see out of the window. He just spends all the time at the window, if I let him. Do you think it's claustrophobia?'

But Jerry knew exactly what it was: Roly was waiting for him to come home from school. He had always been Jerry's dog. He couldn't understand why Jerry wasn't with him now. John would put the receiver next to Roly's ear, and he'd go mad when he heard Jerry's voice, staring all round the room and barking excitedly. John wouldn't do it every week, because he said it took so long to calm him down.

Jerry had forgotten all about his letter to Amelia by the time her reply arrived:

'Dear Jerry, I got your letter. My friends wondered who on earth you were. Sorry you had that trouble about your dog, but he was a bit wild, wasn't he? I know what it's like, though. My first year at St. Patrick's they wouldn't even let me keep Jezabelle here. School is boring as ever. Roll on the hols. Do write. Amelia.'

Jerry read the letter several times, as if looking for something that wasn't there. Then he slowly tore it into small pieces and threw them in the wastepaper bin.

The term dragged on. John said he would come down at half-term with Roly, but at the last minute he couldn't make it. Amelia didn't come either. Then there were the end-of-year exams. Jerry worked hard for these, but he'd missed a lot of the course-work because the school he'd been to in

Coventry did different syllabuses. Also, he developed a persistent illness. He couldn't keep down anything he ate, and he had a bad headache. For virtually a week he had nothing but water. The doctor said it was a virus, but the pills didn't seem to do anything except make Jerry feel sick and dizzy. In the end it went away as mysteriously as it had come. But his exam results weren't good.

Term ended at last in the third week in July, and it had been arranged that on the following Friday John would drive over with Roly, collect Jerry and have him to stay in Coventry for a week. Jerry's parents had to go somewhere at the weekend so it fitted in with their plans and Jerry was overjoyed at the prospect of seeing Roly again. The weather had turned sultry, with an unchanging blanket of thick clouds. On Tuesday the heat drove Jerry out of the house, but there wasn't a breath of air moving in the garden to give any relief.

Wilf was out there, stripped to the waist, harvesting his vegetables. He tossed Jerry a few beans. 'Try them,' he said. 'Broad beans, fresh from the pod! Nothing like 'em . . . Oh! . . . I've got a bit of news that'll interest you. Miss Amelia's coming down at the weekend.'

Jerry looked up, savouring the bitter taste. 'I won't be here.'

Wilf looked puzzled. 'Where are you off to then?'

'Coventry – to see Roly!'

'Oh! Well . . . she'll be staying on a few weeks, no doubt. It's for the cub-hunting. The first hunt's on Sunday.'

'Cub-hunting? What's that?'

'Hunting fox-cubs! The ones that were born in March.'

'What do they want to do that for?' Wilf wiped the sweat

98

from his forehead.

'Come and sit down a minute. This heat takes all the energy out of you.' They went over and sat on a short wooden bench at the back of the house.

'Now then,' he wheezed. 'What do you want to know?'

'Why they hunt fox-cubs. I've never heard of that.'

'They don't broadcast it around, I can tell you, what with all the opposition there is about these days. But there's plenty of reasons for it: number one – it gets the foxes used to running, right? A hunt's no good if the fox just lies in a ditch and gets caught. What they like is a good chase. So – you hunt out the cubs to get 'em into training, sort of thing. Number two – you trains your new entry of hounds at the same time. They got to learn when to call and when to keep quiet, obey all the orders of the Master or Whipper-in . . .'

'What's a Whipper-in?'

'Just what he sounds like. He whips in stray hounds, keeps 'em together in a pack. And number three, it trains your young huntsmen at the same time . . . like Miss Amelia . . . she'll probably get blooded on Sunday . . .'

'Blooded?'

'You know . . . in at the kill . . . they smear the fox's blood on your face . . .'

Jerry was silent. 'I think it's all *stupid*,' he said at last.

'So do a lot of folk,' said Wilf. 'On the other hand, there's a lot that likes it. Packham's one.'

'He's never riding, is he?' asked Jerry.

'Ay!' Wilf chuckled. 'They wanted to ban him, on account of that wolfhound – but seeing as it's mostly his land there's not a lot they can do . . . but he don't ride with the hunt really . . . he just sort of daps about making a nuisance of himself, trying to flush out foxes on his own.'

'Don't they bash all the crops down?'

'They would . . . only they'll be cut. That's why it's on Sunday – by then the farmers'll have everything in.' He squinted at the overcast sky. 'They'll be hurrying too, before this damn weather breaks.'

But the close weather continued on Tuesday and Wednesday. Jerry had been expecting John to ring about the arrangements and nagged his mum into letting him ring John on Wednesday evening. At first there was no reply, but later he got a harrassed-sounding John on the line.

'Hi!' said Jerry. 'It's me. About Roly, and all that.'

'Oh! Look . . . there's a problem,' said John. Jerry's heart began to sink towards his boots.

'What's the matter?'

'It's Roly . . . he's gone off somewhere . . . I've been everywhere.'

'Oh no! When?'

'Yesterday sometime. I didn't want to worry you . . . he was tied up, too . . . somehow he got the knot undone with his mouth. I've been to every police station, Jerry, and the RSPCA. Nobody's seen a whisker of him . . .' Jerry's mum had come up – he gave her the receiver with a shaking hand, and sat down. Roly might have been taken by anybody who took a fancy to him, or perhaps he'd been run down and his body thrown over a hedge.

Jerry went and flung himself on his bed. This new shock and disappointment was almost too much to bear. He felt empty and sick. His mum came up and tried to reassure him that Roly would soon be found, but there wasn't much point in his going to see John until he was. So the visit was postponed until Roly could be found. Jerry would have to look after himself on Saturday while his parents were away. It was as if Jerry had wads of cotton wool in his ears. All he knew was that Roly had gone off looking for him. It was John's fault for not tying him securely – even John had let him down.

On Thursday the heat was worse if anything. Jerry had a headache and stayed in his room listening to the distant roar of the combine harvesters. There was a peculiar fly in the window. It made a very thin buzzing like a dentist's drill that rose higher and higher, until it suddenly cut out. Jerry thought it was being strangled by a spider, but it did the same thing over and over again, the needle-sharp sound penetrating into his brain. In the end he nearly broke the window in a furious attack on it.

He hated the Gatehouse . . . the dull, faded wallpaper, the poky little rooms, the stains and places where the plaster was cracking . . . the worn carpets – nothing theirs but a few pieces of furniture they'd brought, looking shabby in this setting.

On Friday he mooched about the house, afraid to go out in case some news of Roly came through. He wandered from room to room, picking up books and putting them down unread, cursing the minute thunder-bugs which tickled his skin, his mind dull and listless. Finally his mum lost her temper with him.

'You've got to stop this, Jerry!' she cried. 'It's throwing a cloud over everything.'

'Well, what am I supposed to do? Laugh?'

'You've been in mourning for that dog long enough – I sometimes think we'd have done better to sell him!'

'Mum!'

'Well – look, you've got to snap out of it and make the best of things. It's holidays now. I'm not having you traipsing round the house like a lost soul, getting under my feet for the next six weeks. You've got all this lovely countryside round about to explore.'

'Have I?'

'What do you mean by that?'

'It's not *mine* to explore, is it?'

'No!' she shouted. 'It's God's countryside! That's the truth of it! It's Him that made it.'

His dad lowered his newspaper.

'Leave the lad alone,' he said. 'You know what ails him.'

'It's all right for you. You can go off all day. I've told you, I'm not having it. Oh! I can't take much more of this . . .' Her face suddenly crumpled and she ran out of the room. Mr Mills sighed and went after her. Jerry went to his room and assumed his usual position, staring out of the window, head on his arms. In the afternoon he heard a car and from the landing window saw the red Volvo going up the drive. So Amelia had arrived.

He decided to go to the *Windrush*, not because Amelia might turn up there. He didn't care whether he saw her or not. He was astonished at how overgrown it had become in the weeks since he'd been there. He thought there might be a breeze at the tree-top and climbed to the crow's-nest. But even there not a breath of air stirred. The fields shimmered slightly in the heat. In the far distance a red combine harvester crawled rapidly up and down, sending a cloud of dust and flying chaff into the air. Jerry dozed all through the afternoon, jerking awake at intervals to scan all around.

But Amelia didn't come.

Jerry's parents were off early in the morning next day. They told him not to expect them back until very late as they had a long trip – he was to put himself to bed at a reasonable time and not to worry John with phone calls about Roly. The heat was stifling, a close heat that made everything damp, the air thick as soup. Once again he hung around the house most of the day hoping for a telephone call about Roly, but in the end he couldn't stand it and went out to the wood in the late afternoon. He found himself at the spot by the ride where he'd first seen Amelia and sat down there with his back against a tree. Perhaps she'd be going for a ride this evening. The woods were silent, apart from the occasional claxon call of a pheasant and the heavy background hum of insects. He noticed a sweet scent in the air and realised that a nearby bush was a huge rambling honeysuckle. He fell into a kind of trance, with the sensation that he was gradually being turned to stone. Hours passed. A large pale moth hovered at the blossoms, like a humming-bird. Jerry felt paralysed, as if the power to act had been taken from him. All he could do was wait on others to act, follow instructions and wait. And now he couldn't move. He was fixed to the tree. Even his breathing was so light and shallow it was hardly perceptible.

It was almost dark when there came a low rumbling sound in the distance. Jerry stood up without thinking. Thunder!

At the same moment he had come to a decision. He would go up to Battlefields to try to catch a glimpse of Amelia. He didn't even know if she was definitely there. Perhaps she'd been prevented from making contact with him.

103

When he emerged from the wood, lightning was flickering in the clouds along the horizon and the grumbling of thunder came from all directions. He cut across the stubble fields, keeping closer to the hedgerows as he approached the dark pile of the house and the black trees framing it. His heart beat faster. He had to keep the house between himself and Brutus to avoid being detected. He crossed the field bordering the garden and made out the towering shape of the cedar tree. Lights were on in the main room downstairs. There were two lighted windows upstairs also. The whole front of the house was dimly starred with the blooms of a climbing rose.

He decided to make a dash across the lawn. If he could get to the house-wall he could edge along until he could see into the lighted room. He looked over his shoulder. The strange lightning was playing low in the sky like search-lights, but he knew it wasn't bright enough to be a danger to him. He climbed the fence and crept along in the deep shadows of some bushes until he was opposite an unlighted wing of the house. Then he launched himself on to the lawn.

Half-way across something tripped him and sent him sprawling on the grass. He lay still, hardly daring to breathe. Was this a trip-wire which set off a burglar alarm? But there were no sounds of alarm bells or unusual noises from the house. He groped about, and then realised what it was. A croquet hoop stuck in the lawn! He set off again, on hands and knees, gained the terrace and dashed across it to the house-wall. Flattening himself against it, he edged cautiously along until he came to the french windows of a darkened room. He was moving past them towards the lights at the end of the terrace when there was a noise from inside. He froze. The light clicked on, sending a shaft across his path. Suddenly the window was flung open.

'Stuffy in here!' It was Captain Packham's voice. He was so close Jerry could hear his rasping breath. He pressed himself against a stone pillar, hardly daring to breathe. He was trapped. He couldn't go forward or back without passing a lighted window. Packham had moved away and Jerry listened to him shuffling about. Very slowly, a fraction of an inch at a time, he moved his head until he could see into the room.

It was very large, taken up with a full-sized billiard table, on which some kind of military board-game was spread out. A green shuttered light hung low over the table so that the edges of the room were in shadow. Packham was bending over the table staring at the board. Finally he shoved a little group of model tanks and missiles forward with a sort of pusher on a cane. He was wearing his blue naval uniform, with gold buttons and epaulettes. Suddenly there was a louder rumble of thunder. Packham raised his head and cocked it on one side – the odd angle and the light catching the rims of his pale eyes made him look quite insane.

'Your move!' he said sharply. Jerry started. In the shadows at the end of the room was a man. He was in some sort of uniform too, sitting stiffly in a high-backed armchair watching the game. So still and silent was he that Jerry hadn't noticed him. Packham laughed.

'Got you!' he said. 'I thought that out over dinner . . . and you've used up all your reinforcements!'

The man didn't answer, or even move.

Packham hobbled over to the sideboard and poured himself a drink in a big balloon glass. He swilled the liquor round and round thoughtfully.

'Come on, Archie,' he said suddenly. 'Surrender!'

He put the glass down on the edge of the table and went over to the man. He stood looking down at him for a moment. Then, with a swift and totally unexpected movement, he plucked off the officer's hat and replaced it with his own. Jerry suddenly realised. The man wasn't real. It was just a uniform draped over some cushions on the chair. Packham was playing against himself.

Packham returned to the table and put on the officer's hat. He stared at the board for a long time, his mouth working. There was a loud clap of thunder.

'Oh . . . what's the point?' he said savagely and swept the tanks and missiles off the table with his cane, so violently that he lost his balance. His hand came down on the brandy glass, which broke and rolled over the edge, smashing to pieces on the floor. Packham brought his hand up to his mouth, his face twisted with pain.

'Damn! . . . damn!' he muttered.

There was a knock on the door. He straightened up and thrust his cut hand into his jacket pocket.

'Here!' he shouted. 'Who is it?'

The door opened and Amelia came in. Jerry hardly recognised her. She had had her hair cut short, making her face look quite different. Rather plump.

'Gramps! Are you all right? I heard something.'

''Course I'm all right. Just the bloody glass . . .'

'Oh . . . I'll clear it up.'

'Never mind, never mind. Get to bed.'

She turned to go, then stopped. 'Are you riding tomorrow?' she asked.

Packham stared at her, breathing hard. 'Of course I am.'

'Are you sure it isn't too soon?'

'Are you sure I'm not too old, you mean,' he said slowly, almost snarling.

She stared back at him. 'No, Gramps. I didn't mean that. Well, good-night then.'

She went out. Jerry drew back. He felt that he had seen too much. He just wanted to get away from there as fast as he could.

Jerry peeped again. Packham was wrapping a handkerchief round his cut hand. This was Jerry's chance. He edged out along the shadow of the wall pillar which fell across the terrace. Then he heard a sudden movement inside the room and stopped. Very slowly, he turned his head to look back. Packham had come to the window and seemed to be staring straight out at him. Jerry held his breath. Packham took a comb from his pocket and began to comb his hair.

Jerry realised that he was looking at himself in the window. He stared, hypnotised, as Packham drew himself up and studied his reflection. Suddenly he had the weird sensation that he *was* Packham's reflection . . . that he'd been taken over by him completely . . . that he was paralysed and couldn't move unless Packham did . . .

Then Packham straightened his tie and pulled his face into an imitation grin, and for a split second Jerry knew what it was like to be him and felt sorry for him. But next moment there was a brilliant flash of lightning. The fake grin turned to a look of horror. Jerry didn't wait. He knew he'd been seen. He ran for it, with Packham's cry ringing in his ears.

Within a few minutes Jerry was back at the Gatehouse. His parents weren't home yet. He didn't dare turn on the lights. He stood in the dark living-room, straining his ears for sounds of pursuit. He had heard shouts and Brutus baying as he raced down the drive. Had he been recognised? He ran upstairs and looked fearfully out of the landing window, dreading to see car headlights approaching. There weren't any, but it seemed to him there were more lights of some sort, shining through the trees. If Packham had recognised him he would come to the house, maybe with Brutus . . . and Jerry was alone. His parents might not be back for ages. He couldn't stay there. Packham had a key to the house . . . he feverishly began to collect a few things together in a rucksack: sweater, anorak, sleepingbag, some bread and cheese – it was difficult finding things in the darkness and he kept breaking off to peer through the window. At the door he hesitated. Should he leave a note for his parents? He didn't even know where he was going. In a flash the image of the *Windrush* came to him. He would spend the night there. But where could he leave a note? He tried to think clearly. Packham could get into the house – he could search anywhere – it was his house. There was no private place that was safe from him. Jerry couldn't risk it. He quietened his breathing and listened again. Suddenly the telephone began to ring, sounding deafeningly loud in the silent house. He knew instantly that it was Packham. He was paralysed with fear. Then he realised that it might be his parents, but he didn't want to find out. He grabbed his rucksack and raced out of the house and up the lane at top speed.

It was a strange night. The air smelt sharp and fresh as lemons. His body felt alert, as if woken from a long sleep. It was pitch dark, save for the frequent flashes of lightning, showing a colourless dream landscape. It reminded him of somebody taking black and white photographs with a flash-bulb; photographs of him perhaps, bounding silently, almost flying above the ground.

Once in the fields he slowed down. There seemed to be no wind, yet every tree he passed was making a continuous low hissing noise, as if all the leaves were trembling slightly. These trees were black against a sky of darkest grey. He began to see them as shapes: the enormous head of a girl with a pony-tail, in profile, holding up a mirror and staring fixedly into it; a huge military boot, probably several low trees bunched together with a very big one; and, as he climbed a slope, a dark mass of foliage hanging over the skyline became the great head of a wolf, resting on its paws, a couple of grey chinks glinting through the dark leaves, like eyes. He imagined the thunder was its furious growling.

He was glad to get into the deeper darkness of the wood, where he was invisible. But here there were other things: a series of gasping rattles, like the wheezy breaths of an old man, repeated at intervals. It must have been a bird, but no bird Jerry had ever heard before. Then a harsh scream that died away into a bubbling gargle, and sudden rustlings as of creatures moving stealthily in the undergrowth. Jerry fought against panic, straining to see a path by the intermittent flashes of lightning, and forcing himself not to start running. He imagined the Levellers fleeing in terror through this wood pursued by Cromwell's men, crashing fearlessly after them with guns firing. He made himself move slowly, groping forward like a blind man. Suddenly something big got up almost under his feet and crashed away into the bushes. He stood shivering for a long time, straining to see into the darkness, listening for every whisper of sound.

Finally he was able to go on. The ground became more open as he mounted to the ridge, and then he was descending again. He scrambled through the barbed wire fence marking the boundary of Packham's land and was soon on the banks of the stream, smelling the wet moss and water-weed. Everything looked different at night. The island was just a dark mass, with the black column of the pine rising from it. He found his drawbridge where he'd left it concealed in the bushes and, taking advantage of the lightning, crossed over the stream.

He unrolled the sleeping-bag and lay down with the rucksack under his head, listening to the chuckling stream, letting the thick darkness press on his eyes. It was good in the cabin – for the first time he felt safe.

He felt the security of an animal deep in its burrow. Nobody would find him here. But he wasn't sleepy and after a while he got up on deck, and climbed to the crow's-nest.

The familiar view of rolling tree-tops on the one hand and fields on the other was transformed into mysterious contours of black and grey, except when briefly and starkly lit by the glare of lightning. He smelled the sweet pine resin on his fingers and settled himself comfortably back into the notch of branches. The words of a song his brother had repeatedly played when he'd come to fetch Roly, came into his mind:

'I'm leavin' my family
I'm leavin' all my friends
My body's at home, but my heart's in the wind . . .'

There was a brilliant flash. A tendril of lightning snaked down over the distant hills. He counted to seven before the loud crash of thunder followed. Seven miles away. The electricity in the air had concentrated itself into a definite thunderstorm.

He closed his eyes. The trees were all hissing like surf on a shingle beach. There was a fine mist in the air. In his mind the *Windrush* swung clear of the harbour mouth and out into the open sea, her prow cutting steadily through the water. He was leaving all the trouble – heading for a new land where nobody knew him:

'So swallow me, don't follow me
Travelling alone
blue water's my daughter
I'm gonna skip like a stone . . .
And nobody knows me
I can't fathom my stay
And shiver me timbers
I'm sailing away . . .'

The next flash was so bright he could see it through closed

111

eyelids. He counted to five before the thunder came with a clap that jerked him upright. The storm was moving his way. For the first time he thought of the danger. The pine was the tallest tree in that part of the wood and must be a likely target. The wind was rising, and the tree began to sway and creak. With a feeling of reckless daring he decided to wait for one more flash before climbing down.

It came as a crackling sheet of light from which two jagged bolts, like nerve pathways on fire, lashed down in the middle distance, illuminating the fields round about. Jerry started violently. He'd seen something in one of those fields, glimpsed it for only a split second before everything was plunged into darkness again. He'd forgotten to count, but the thunder came only a few seconds later, seeming to shake the very tree with its force. He stood up, gripping the branches, straining forward to see what it was, when the next flash came.

He didn't have long to wait. The whole sky blazed with searing light and in that momentary brilliance he saw it again: smaller than a sheep, hunched against the storm, moving slowly from the direction of the main road.

'Oh please . . . please,' whispered Jerry, ignoring the deafening thunder.

'Please let it be . . .' The first big drops of rain began to fall. He leaned forward precariously to see better, when the next bolt came.

Jerry didn't see that bolt. It came snickering down behind him to touch an oak on the crest of the ridge. But in its glare he saw the field, saw the white animal limping across it and into the ear-splitting crash of thunder, which came simultaneously, he yelled with all the force of his lungs.

112

'ROLEEEEEE!' The thunder died away. He scrambled desperately down the tree, shouting the dog's name over and over again into the lashing rain. And as he slid, spinning, down the wet rope, he heard an answering bark.

They met in the shallows below the island, dancing round each other in the water; Roly yelping and barking, Jerry shouting his name hoarsely, with the rain pouring over them and the storm raging around. Finally, exhausted, Jerry crawled on to the *Windrush*, while Roly took a long drink from the stream. Then he carried Roly to the cabin, dropped him in and lowered himself after. The overhanging bank sheltered it from the rain and his gear was still dry. He stripped off his wet clothes and dried Roly with his spare sweater. He'd forgotten to bring a towel. But he got himself reasonably dry and crawled into the sleeping bag. Roly lay across it, nuzzling his legs. He put his arm round Roly's neck, and buried his face in his fur.

'They're not going to send you away again,' he said softly. 'I won't let them. Maybe we'll have to live in the woods, eat fish and rabbits and pigeons, be like outlaws . . . It won't be stealing. Those things don't belong to anyone . . . they belong to themselves. Like you, Roly, you don't belong to me.' Roly whined. 'No, it's true, you don't. We're just together here, now, because we want to be. That's right, Roly. That's how it is.' He frowned into the darkness. 'Even the ground belongs to itself. People think they own it, but they don't. They just pass through it.' He patted Roly's head, sighed and fell asleep.

10 Jerry woke at dawn. For a few seconds he stared at the watery patterns of sunlight reflected on to the earth-roof of the cabin, not knowing where he was. Then he heard the softly snoring dog and remembered. He sat up on one elbow and stared at Roly in amazement. He had a bad scratch on one side and a cut on one of his paws. But he'd made it, over forty miles across country. Jerry had heard of cats and dogs being able to do this, but it was impossible to understand. He wondered if they navigated by sun or stars and what happened when they came to an obstacle like a river, or a town?

'You're fantastic, Roly,' he said quietly. The green drapes of foliage moved slightly in the breeze. A fly buzzed around the cabin. He listened to the stream and felt a deep contentment. Roly had come back and he wouldn't let them send him away again. The dog was obviously exhausted by his journey. Very quietly, so as not to wake him, Jerry climbed up on deck and spread his clothes on some bushes to dry. He ate the bread and cheese which he'd brought from the house and wondered what he could give Roly to eat. He didn't like bread and cheese. He liked blackberries, but they weren't ripe.

Slowly Jerry's thoughts began to cloud. He thought of the trouble waiting for him, furious parents, and Packham . . . His mind flinched from the memory of his crazy visit to Battlefields. Perhaps he hadn't been recognized . . . perhaps Packham had only seen a vague outline for a split second . . . He would have to face them sooner or later. He became conscious of a feeling of dread, lurking at the back of his mind throughout everything that had happened.

A faint sound came floating over the fields, something like a distant car-horn. He rapidly climbed to the crow's-nest and scanned all around. There was nobody in sight. It was a beautiful clear morning, with huge white clouds in the sky, and the tree-tops rolling slowly in the wind. The sound came again from the direction of the fields, a confused murmur and the faintest possible musical note, like a trumpet. He stood up and craned over the branches to see. Then he saw it. A tiny flash of brilliant red – and the sound turned into the distant clamour of barking dogs. The cub-hunt! He'd forgotten all about it.

He could see them now, streaming down a hillside a couple of miles away: a straggle of hounds, black and tan with white flashes; and then the horses, only about a dozen, one of which was a grey. No doubt this was Amelia. Jerry wondered if Packham was with them and stirred uneasily. The hounds poured into a large covert about four fields distant. One of the huntsmen headed off strays. Jerry could hear shouts and the faint snapping of a whip. The huntsmen gathered at the edges of the covert, waiting to see what the hounds would flush out. He wondered if there were fox-cubs in there, cowering in terror under bushes or creeping into a ditch, not sure whether to sit tight or make a run for

115

it. He hoped they wouldn't come any nearer, but suddenly one of the hounds broke out of the copse, baying loudly, heading straight towards him. He looked down, moving to begin descending the tree, then froze. A fox was trotting down the bank of the stream, below the island. This was no cub, but a fully-grown fox. Jerry was sure it was the same one that had raided the chicken run.

The fox seemed perfectly calm. He stopped at the water's edge and took a drink, occasionally glancing over his shoulder in the direction of the hunt. Then he crossed the shallows, leaping from stone to stone, and went up the bank to the hole which Roly had investigated so thoroughly on their first visit. Jerry glanced back at the hunt. The dogs were crossing a stubble-field in full cry, perhaps half a mile away. He looked down again.

The fox hadn't gone to earth. He was retracing his steps carefully back to the stream. Once there, he slipped into the water and swam steadily up past the island and out of sight. In a flash Jerry understood. The fox had laid a false scent. The dogs would follow the trail to the hole and think it had gone to earth. While they were trying to dig it out, the fox would escape up-river, its scent concealed by the water. Then he realised something else. The fox had led the hunt to hideout. In a few minutes the whole place would be swarming with dogs and riders. They'd be sure to find the *Windrush* and Roly . . . and him.

His heart racing, Jerry shinned down the tree, jumping the last ten feet and calling to Roly as soon as he hit the ground. Frantically he put on his sneakers and bundled his wet things into the cabin. He couldn't carry all this stuff with him – he would just have to risk it being found. Roly

116

jumped out of the cabin into the stream and swam round to the shallows below the island. Jerry looked at his bedraggled appearance and remembered the cut paw. If the hunt picked up that scent it might follow them instead of the fox. He had to use the same trick. He plunged into the water, then stopped. The flag! If only he'd torn it down when he was climbing down the tree. But there was no time left. The baying was suddenly louder and he could distinctly hear the thunder of hooves. They must be in the field bordering the wood. Jerry looked downstream. The first bend was a good twenty metres away.

'Come on, Roly,' he called urgently, and raced for the bend. Within a few yards the stream narrowed again and the water deepened. He ran as far as he could, then flung himself forward and struck out with all his strength. Roly gamely followed and in a few moments the current swept them round the bend.

They were just in time. As Jerry allowed himself to be carried along under the high banks, he heard splashing and loud yelps. The first hounds had reached the water and were milling round in a frenzy of excitement. With fresh panic, he struck out again, urging Roly to follow. He had to get out of earshot of the hunt before he cut into the wood to find a hiding place. It was impossible here anyway. The wood had turned into a swamp, with thin scraggy trees poking out of pools of black mud. The stream became sluggish, almost choked in some places with reeds and water lilies. Fronds of weed curled round his ankles. He looked round anxiously at Roly. He was obviously unhappy, swimming repeatedly towards the banks and then veering away from the reeds. Jerry knew he was exhausted from his

117

long journey, and was terrified he'd get entangled in the water-weed. The sounds of the hunt were muffled now. He was not being followed it seemed, and he looked urgently for a place to get out.

The stream twisted and turned, and he saw with relief that the ground was drier on the wood side, and round the next bend, the stream widened into a pool with a high bank on the field side. Opposite was a sand-bank and beyond it a steep but climbable bank, with plenty of cover on top. He scrambled on to the sand-bank and hauled Roly up after him. He was shivering, and had trouble getting up the bank. Jerry had to drag him over the top by his collar. They both collapsed on the ground gasping for breath.

Suddenly Roly stiffened and growled oddly. Jerry followed his gaze across the stream, and froze with horror. They were being watched. Stock-still on the opposite bank stood a huge black horse. The rider was staring at them with a look of cold hatred.

'It's the little spy,' said Captain Packham quietly. Jerry scrambled to his feet.

'I warned you,' said Packham. He lowered his head towards where Brutus was standing rigid at the horse's side and, keeping his eyes fixed on Jerry and Roly, pointed with his whip.

'Go on, boy,' he hissed. 'Get 'em!' A wave of terror swept over Jerry. Even as Brutus sprang forward he turned and ran into the wood. But Roly was ahead of him, a white shadow darting among the trees, somehow finding a path through the hopeless tangle of brambles and fallen rotting wood. Jerry ran as he'd never run in any school sprint, leaping the ditches like a stag, smashing through bushes and

118

briars, dodging the whippy branches. He heard the splash as Brutus hit the water. How much start did he have? He forced his whirling brain to think. Thirty seconds maybe, for him to swim the pool and climb the bank. Jerry put on a spurt, but his water-logged shoes and wet clothes slowed him down. He was running for his life. He pictured the long spidery legs of the wolfhound bounding, loping after them, gaining steadily with its long stride. And now he heard it – the grating triumphant howl of the hound on the blood trail. Brutus was in the wood. Jerry could climb a tree, but not Roly. There was no chance of lifting his six and a half stone up with him.

He ran flat out as he'd never run before, but in his heart he knew it was hopeless. His legs felt like lead, his lungs near to bursting, his body became a blur of pain. He was flagging. And running was becoming almost impossible. There were no paths. The spaces between the trees were clogged with half-fallen poles and brambles. They seemed to be closing in around him, dense briars on either side, and arching overhead; until he was stumbling bent double, down a kind of tunnel. Behind him the baying came louder and louder, until his panic-stricken mind could only repeat the word 'Help!' over and over again. He wanted to lie down and die, but terror kept him going. Then a low branch struck his face, hard. He dropped to his knees gasping and moaning, but scrambled forward, on all fours, like Roly.

A few seconds later he crashed into Roly. He had stopped, and Jerry, blinded by sweat, hadn't seen him. He wiped his eyes. In front of him was a wall of briars so thick that not even a dog could get through. On his right were matted thorn bushes, worse, if anything. On the left, a dense

119

bed of nettles, higher than his head. He forced himself to stop breathing and listen. With a sob he recognised the sound of Brutus pattering through the undergrowth, maybe only twenty metres away. He dived into the nettles, hardly feeling the stinging prickles on his face and hands.

Suddenly he was free of them. He opened his eyes and stared around. He was on the edge of a small pond, hidden among the trees. In a flash, he remembered it. Primordial Pond, where he'd found the moorhen's nest so long ago. Could he get into the water? Would Brutus attack them there? But one look at Roly told him this was no good. He would probably drown. He had collapsed on the ground, shivering violently and panting hard. Desperately he looked round. Then he remembered it. The pipe in the hillside! His mind worked furiously. If he could get into the pipe with Roly and jam up the entrance with branches they might be safe. With his last shreds of strength he hauled Roly by the collar up the slope. There was the pipe among thick brambles. Desperately he pushed Roly inside, and cast around for something to barricade the entrance. As he did so the blunt muzzle of the wolfhound burst out of the nettles. Jerry watched fascinated as Brutus stopped at the edge of the pond, sniffing the ground where Roly had collapsed. Then he looked up, straight at Jerry. His lip curled back in a vicious snarl and he sprang forward.

With a cry of despair, Jerry seized a huge armful of brambles, not even feeling the lacerating thorns, tore it free of the ground and backed into the pipe, dragging it after him. The pipe was only just large enough for him to enter on hands and knees. He scrabbled backwards and the brambles compressed into a solid ball as he dragged them in after him. Hardly had he wedged them in when there was a pattering of feet and the grey spidery shape of the wolfhound blotted out the light. Brutus flung himself against the barrier. Jerry screamed at the top of his lungs. Brutus checked, and backed away pawing angrily at his head.

Jerry scuttled backwards and lay on the floor of the pipe. Long shudders of terror racked his body. Brutus came at the barrier again, but the small compass of the pipe meant that he couldn't launch himself at it properly. Jerry watched him shoving his head into the brambles again and again. He knew he could do no more. If Brutus got through, he was at his mercy. But the thorns stabbing at his muzzle and eyes defeated him, and after half a dozen attempts, he sat back on his haunches and howled for his master. The sound echoed eerily down the pipe and sent a new wave of horror through him. Packham would come. Jerry was trapped in the pipe, with only the briars between himself and a murderous wolfhound. Packham would pull them out. It would be murder. But Packham was insane. He would do it. Jerry stuffed his fist in his mouth to stop himself screaming. Who would know? Packham would say it was an accident. He'd blame it on the dog. Nobody would doubt his word. Nobody would suspect it was deliberate murder. He'd get away with it. Brutus would be put down, but Packham would get away with it. He fought to control rising hysteria. To think. Where did the pipe go? He twisted round and looked over his shoulder. Roly was lying a few metres further up, completely done in. Beyond him the pipe seemed to slope upwards into pitch darkness. Yet the water had to come from somewhere. Jerry began to crawl backwards on hands and knees, pushing Roly gently with his feet. The entrance dwindled to the size of a coin.

Suddenly he stopped breathing. Was it the thumping of blood in his ears, or was it hoof-beats? The drumming got louder. A few particles of dirt fell on his upturned face. It was a horse. Packham's horse, above him somewhere on the hill.

'Oh God!' whispered Jerry. 'No, no.' He scrabbled backwards faster through the icy water, further and further up the slimy dank-smelling pipe, with black despair in his heart. He stopped. There was an obstacle – some sort of blockage. A mound of fallen debris filled the pipe. The drumming hoof-beats ceased. A dark shape blotted out the little disc of light and Packham's insane laugh echoed down the pipe.

'Gone to earth, eh?' He heard the sound he'd dreaded – the scraping of brambles being pulled out of the entrance. Somewhere behind him Roly whined. Jerry groped out to comfort him. But he wasn't there. He twisted around, then understood. There was a faint light, a small gap at the top of the mound. Somehow Roly had squeezed through. Jerry lay out at full length and wriggled backwards up the mound. He got his feet through the gap, shoving himself along with his hands. He forced his hips through, but his shoulders jammed. He sobbed a prayer and twisted savagely, clawing at the debris. Suddenly he was through. He looked over his shoulder. There was a greenish light. Only a few feet away was the end of the pipe choked with grass and nettles. Roly was peering in at him. Just then came the booming howl of Brutus, echoing strangely as he clambered up the pipe.

Jerry frantically scooped handfuls of mud and stones and

122

shoved them up into the gap he'd crawled through. Then he backed out and stood on shaky legs. They were out of the wood. The river Windrush curled peacefully along the foot of the hill. There was the ford and beyond it the track that led home.

If the blockage held . . . maybe they could just make it. 'Come on, Roly,' he gasped, as a furious snarling and scrabbling told him that Brutus had reached the mound. He half-ran, half-fell down the hill on legs that didn't seem to belong to him. Roly limped after him and Jerry had to repeatedly urge him on. If he could just get to the top of the slope beyond the river, they'd almost be in sight of the Gatehouse . . . Packham wouldn't dare . . .

But he didn't get that far. He was half-way across the ford when there was a triumphant baying from behind them. Jerry forced himself to look back. Brutus was out of the pipe and tearing down the hill with great loping strides. Roly twisted round and lost his footing on the wet stones. The current swirled him downstream. Jerry plunged after him and managed to grab his collar, just round the first bend. He dragged him ashore, on to a little stony beach. They were hidden from the ford by the bend in the river, but Jerry knew Brutus would find them. He staggered to the high bank, behind the beach, and turned with his back against it. There was nowhere left to run.

11 There was a pattering rush of paws on wet stones. Brutus came hurtling round the corner. His body seemed almost to twist in mid-air as he caught sight of Jerry and crashed down in the shallows, only a couple of metres away. Saliva dripped from his great jaws. His eyes were shadows in the bristling grey fur. He laid back his ears and curled his thin lip. Jerry fell back against the bank. Brutus paused, as if sensing that he had Jerry at his mercy. He bared his old yellow teeth in a snarl.

But there was an answering snarl. Something shot past Jerry like a white bolt. Brutus was taken by surprise. Roly's six and a half stone hit him with the force of a battering ram. He went for the throat, but at the last moment Brutus managed to turn slightly and Roly's teeth sank deep into his left shoulder. The impact bowled Brutus right over and for a moment he struggled frantically in the shallow water, seeming to be at Roly's mercy. He lay floundering on his side, legs beating the air. Then somehow he regained his footing and rose to his full height, towering above Roly, whose limp body swung this way and that as Brutus tried to shake him off.

124

But Roly hung on, jaws clamped like a vice, and Brutus couldn't get his head round far enough to bite him. He seemed to go insane. He whirled and twisted and rotated until he was a blur of snarling snapping fury. Still Roly hung on. Then they were down again, rolling over and over in the water, churning it into a welter of foam.

'Roly,' whispered Jerry, shaking so much he could hardly stand. Brutus was staggering crazily now, half-leaping and somehow lifting Roly with him, thrashing, floundering and howling all the while with insane fury. It looked as if his utmost strength could not dislodge Roly. But he found the way. Lying on his side, he somehow managed to draw up his legs and raked his claws savagely across Roly's belly, cutting deep into the soft flesh. Roly yowled with pain and released his grip. Brutus sprang away. He shook his great blunt head a few times. His wet fur clung to him like a threadbare rug, showing his gaunt muscular frame. His eyes, visible for the first time, were as pitiless as little black stones. He began to circle warily round Roly, looking for an opening to finish him off. Roly turned always to face him, but he was swaying on his feet. Blood flowed freely from the claw wounds, staining the water in spreading red clouds.

The sight of this was too much for Jerry. In sudden uncontrollable rage he picked up a rock from the beach and hurled it at Brutus with all his strength. Guided by the force of desperate will, the rock smashed straight into the snarling jaws of the wolfhound. It was a blow which would have sent most dogs bolting off, whimpering with pain, but not Brutus. It merely diverted his attention from Roly to

125

Jerry. He shook the blood and broken teeth from his mouth and fixed on Jerry a look of utter savage ferocity. This was it. Roly was done for. Jerry was defenceless. He saw Brutus' muscles tighten for the rush. He heard a pounding in his head and a voice screaming somewhere nearby. The pounding got louder and louder. The scream stretched like elastic. What followed seemed like a vision.

A huge black horse came thundering round the corner. Confronted by the dogs or perhaps at the sound of Jerry screaming, it reared up. The rider was thrown backwards, but somehow managed to stay in the saddle.

'YOU!' he screamed, grabbing the saddle. Brutus cringed as if whipped. The horse, staggering on its hind legs, neighing frantically, lost its footing on the slippery stones and fell heavily, crashing down on to the cowering wolfhound. The rider was thrown as the horse fell. He landed face down in the shallow water and lay still. The horse scrambled to its feet and sheered off downstream. Brutus' crushed body floated slowly after it.

Everything went deathly quiet. Jerry felt dull, as if some vital part of his brain wasn't working. He walked unsteadily over to where Packham lay. He looked unreal. One of his arms was twisted the wrong way. Jerry felt awkward, as if he'd come upon a stranger asleep. He bent down and lifted the head out of the water. There was a gargling noise. A trickle of blood and water came out of the mouth. The face was pale, eyes closed.

Suddenly something caught Jerry's eye: a round hat, drifting towards him like a little boat. The scene became familiar, as if he were watching a repeated film: the limp body with the arm twisted back; the strands of grey hair clinging wetly to the scalp, the riding hat, now caught in an eddy, slowly spinning and filling with water.

He stared around stupidly, trying to wake up. His mind cleared and he heard the rippling stream, the birds singing, Roly whimpering.

'Don't worry,' he said to Packham. 'You'll be all right. It doesn't matter.'

He pulled the body out of the water. It was surprisingly frail and easy to lift. He laid it gently on the beach, face down, with the head turned to one side. He bent over and listened. No sound of breathing. He felt the wrist, staring with a kind of horror at the blue veins. There was a pulse, faint but regular. He felt sudden panic. The face was turning slightly blue. What should he do? He tried desperately to remember . . . concussion . . . a drowning man, alive but not breathing . . . he might have inhaled water . . . he had to push it out . . . the kiss of life . . . No, he couldn't do that . . . the other way. He knelt over Packham's thin back and pressed down with the flat of his hands . . . Nothing. He shoved again, harder, and again. A trickle of water came out of the open mouth. Furiously he pushed again and again. Suddenly there was a gush of liquid. Packham gave a shuddering groan and started to breathe.

Jerry rocked back on his heels, gasping, dizzy. He had been holding his breath. Something had happened to his stomach. It felt solid, hard as a rock. The scene began to fade and turn yellowish-brown, like parchment burning up at the edges. He closed his eyes.

'This is silly,' he thought. 'This is silly.' He put his head between his knees and took some deep breaths. Gradually

127

his head cleared. He opened his eyes. Roly had lain down beside him. Absently he fondled his neck, looking at the fallen figure of his enemy. There was no feeling of victory or triumph. Only a pathetic old man, perhaps close to death. Packham was unconscious – maybe he'd been concussed or had a heart attack. His arm was obviously broken. His life might be hanging by a thread. Jerry realised he had to get help. He struggled to his feet. His legs ached with the effort of merely standing up. He couldn't possibly run home. It would be a slow and painful walk. His eye fell on Packham's horse, standing a little way downstream, drinking deeply. The horse! He could ride the horse back home. That would be the fastest way to get help. But he hesitated. He'd never ridden a horse in his life. He remembered when he'd asked Wilf once if it was difficult.

'There's a lot of silly nonsense talked about it,' he said. 'It's just getting on and staying on, like riding a bike. In fact its a lot easier than riding a bike. You haven't got to balance.' Jerry looked at the big animal. Strings of water and saliva fell from its mouth and long shudders ran down its wet flanks. He began to walk slowly towards it. It might not let him ride it. It was Packham's horse. And it was clearly nervous after the fall. He was standing beside it now. The stirrups were at his shoulder level, much too high to get his feet in. He patted it on the neck. It snorted and moved away still shuddering. Very slowly he approached it again, and began to rub its neck and muzzle, talking softly. It permitted this. He took a rein and led it gently over to the bank. Still holding the rein, he scrambled up the bank. When he was high enough he swung across into the saddle. He was mounted. Roly had got to his feet and was watching

Jerry anxiously.

'Stay, Roly,' he called. 'Good boy. Stay here – guard.' He pointed to the figure of Packham. Roly walked over and flopped down beside the body.

'Good boy, Roly! Stay!'

Jerry got his feet into the stirrups, and gave a little kick. The horse moved away from the bank and began to walk downstream. It was a strange sensation. The ground so far away, the swaying motion of the enormously muscular body, the smell of leather harness, and the feeling of moving without effort.

Jerry could see all around. To the left were the fields stretching up to the bluff where Battlefields stood among its guard of trees. When they came to a convenient place he gingerly pulled the left rein. The horse dutifully turned and waded in huge strides through the stream and up the low bank into the water-meadow.

Jerry's heart was beating fast, but he wasn't afraid.

'Come on,' he said, giving a little kick with his heels. He had intended to spur the horse into a slightly faster walk or a slow trot, but it suddenly tossed its head and broke into a canter. Jerry was jerked backwards and very nearly thrown. His feet came out of the stirrups but he hung on to the reins, his wet jeans sticking to the saddle. He gripped as hard as he could with his legs. The horse moved from a canter to a gallop, which was easier to ride. The animal was like some great powerful engine, the hooves thumping with the regularity of pistons. The wind whipped his hair about and made his eyes water. He squinted over the flying mane and saw with sudden alarm that they were heading for a low hedge which ran the length of the field without a break.

129

'Whoa,' he cried, pulling at the reins. 'Slow down, boy!' But the horse jerked its head forward and, if anything, increased its speed. Jerry realised it was going to jump. He looked at the ground flashing past so far below. No, it would be suicide to leap off. The hedge raced towards them. Jerry closed his eyes, and grabbed the saddle. The thrumming hoof-beats ceased. There was a long silence, then a jolt which knocked the breath out of his body and pitched him forward on to the horse's neck. He clung desperately to the mane. The hoof-beats resumed, crackling like fire as the horse raced across a field of stubble. He was still on, somehow. He had come out of the saddle and was partly sprawled along the horse's back. If it had turned he would have fallen in a moment. But it was a huge field and the animal went straight across it, seeming to know its way home.

Jerry eased himself forward inch by inch until he was in the saddle again. But it was impossible to get his feet into the dancing stirrups or catch the flying reins, so he just clung to the saddle boss. A small wood loomed up ahead. He had scarcely got used to the field before the horse dived into a kind of tunnel. Twigs lashed at his head. Trees and bushes flashed by on either side. He buried his face in the mane, not daring to look up. The horse jinked to right and left down the twisting bridle-path. Still he hung on. But he knew he was out of control, on a runaway.

The sound of hooves changed as they emerged from the wood. He risked a glance. Just in time. The track veered sharply to the right. He instinctively leaned inwards as the horse swung round the bend. Suddenly the hooves were pounding on gravel. The long drive to Battlefields stretched out ahead. Jerry sat up a little in the saddle and took a deep breath. They were on the home straight. Somehow, he'd made it. The rhythm of the hooves beat in his ears like drums. He felt like the messenger who rides desperately from the battlefield with news of victory or defeat.

They swung round the big trees and there was the beautiful old house, its golden stone softly glowing in the sunlight. In front of the house stood a police car. Amelia's grey was tied up nearby. The horse slowed to a trot. Jerry felt as if he were riding a pneumatic drill. The front door burst open. Amelia ran down the steps, followed by some grown-ups. Jerry saw his parents and a policeman. Amelia grabbed the horse's bridle and pulled it up. He slumped in the saddle gasping for breath, as the grown-ups gathered round, staring at him in amazement. His sodden, filthy clothes were ripped to rags. Any exposed skin was smeared with dried mud and lacerated by scratches, cuts and welts. His knees and elbows were grazed raw, his hands were bleeding, and his face was puffy with nettle stings. He stared back at the circle of astonished faces. Suddenly his mum wailed and grabbed his leg.

'Jerry – Oh Jerry, what's happened to you? Look at you!'

'I'm all right, Mum,' he gasped. 'It's Captain Packham. He's been thrown!'

12 They all started talking at once. Jerry slid off the horse and half-fell to the ground. The policeman stepped forward.

'Just a minute,' he said loudly. 'Let the lad speak. Did you say somebody was hurt?'

'Yes . . . Captain Packham. He's knocked out . . .'

Mrs Packham gasped. 'Leonard,' she cried. 'I knew something would happen.' Amelia put her arm around her.

'Where is he?' asked the policeman, urgently.

'By the river . . . I can show you.'

'What's the nearest point a vehicle could get to him?' Jerry tried to think.

'There's a track off the lane . . . up towards the main road.'

'Right,' said the policeman, moving rapidly to his car. 'I'll radio for an ambulance on the way.' He turned as everyone followed. 'I can't take you all, you know.'

'I used to be a nurse,' said Mrs Mills. 'Maybe I can do something . . .'

'I'll drive Mrs Packham then,' said Mr Mills. She was obviously too upset to drive herself.

Jerry got in the front and his mum sat in the back of the police car. They sent the gravel flying as he accelerated away down the drive. The policeman took a microphone off the dashboard.

'Foxtrot Bravo 7,' he said. 'Emergency service required, over.' There was a garbled reply. 'Ambulance please . . . Ambulance to Battlefields, urgent . . . That's right. Battlefields House, near Windrush. Don't go to the house – stop in the lane before you get there. You'll see a police car, right?' There was a comment which Jerry couldn't make out.

'Very funny,' said the policeman. 'They want to know who won.'

'Nobody,' said Jerry. His mum leaned forward and put her hand on his shoulder.

'We were that worried about you, Jerry,' she said. 'How on earth did you get into this state?'

'I slept rough . . . in the woods.'

'But . . . you look as if you've been in a fight or something.'

'Hey, Mum . . . I found Roly!'

'What! You never have!'

'He came back . . . all the way from Coventry on his own! I left him guarding Captain Packham.' His mum stared at him in amazement.

'How bad is he?' asked the policeman, as they screeched round Dead Pine Corner.

'I don't know . . . he fell in the stream and breathed some water.'

'How do you know that?'

'Well . . . he stopped breathing, so I did some first aid

133

. . . pressed on his back, and got it out. And he started breathing again.' The policeman glanced at Jerry.

'Good lad . . . and you rode back?'

'Yes . . . I couldn't . . .'

'We could do with a few more like you,' said the policeman.

'Is he bleeding?' asked Jerry's mum.

'No – I don't think so. But I think his arm's broken.'

'Have you got a blanket, or anything we could wrap him in till the ambulance comes?' she asked.

'I've got a blanket in the boot – and a thermos of hot coffee.'

'We best not give him anything to drink,' she said. 'He might need an anaesthetic.'

'There it is!' Jerry pointed to the stile. The police car swerved off the lane and skidded to a halt on the verge. They got out the blanket and set off at a run down the track. Jerry stumbled along as best he could on aching legs and blistered feet.

Captain Packham was lying just as Jerry had left him, with Roly faithfully on guard. The policeman bent over the body and listened.

'He's still alive, thank God,' he said. 'How long is it since the accident?' Jerry tried to work it out, but it was difficult to estimate. So much had happened it felt like hours.

'I'm not sure . . . maybe half an hour or more.' Mrs Mills wrapped Captain Packham in the blanket and rolled him gently on to his side.

'It's a good thing he wasn't lying on his back,' she said. 'He might have suffocated on his tongue.'

'Look!' exclaimed Jerry. 'His eyes moved!' Captain

134

Packham's eyes flickered open. He made a feeble attempt to lift his head, groaned and fell back, staring round wildly.

'Don't try to move, sir,' said the policeman. 'There's help on its way – you've taken a nasty fall.' Captain Packham's lips moved silently. One of his hands twitched. A distant siren came faintly across the fields.

'Won't be long now,' said the policeman. 'There's the ambulance. Just relax. Don't try to talk. You'll soon be in good hands.' As he spoke, Amelia came running up.

'Oh, Gramps!' she cried, bursting into tears.

'Now then, Miss, don't over-excite him,' said the policeman. 'Just talk to him gently.'

The policeman turned to Jerry's mum and began speaking to her in a low voice. Jerry looked at Amelia. She gradually ceased sobbing and wiped her eyes.

'He must have had enough and decided to ride home,' she said at last. 'But where's Brutus?'

'He . . . he's dead,' said Jerry. 'The horse fell on him.' She stared at him wide-eyed.

'Dead?' She looked at Roly. The long gashes on his belly were still bleeding a little. Then she looked back at Jerry's disfigured face, bloody hands and torn and lacerated arms and legs.

'What really happened?' she asked softly. Captain Packham's pale eyes had opened wider and were fixed on Jerry with a peculiar intensity, like those of a wounded hawk.

He hesitated.

'Brutus and Roly got in a fight . . . I . . . I was over by the bank. His horse came charging round the corner and slipped on the stones. It fell on Brutus . . . crushed him.'

He somehow felt ashamed for Packham, as if the chase were a secret between them he ought not to reveal.

'But what was he doing here?' she persisted. 'Why did he . . .?' She stopped as a thought struck her.

'It was an accident,' said Jerry firmly. He looked at Captain Packham. Their eyes met and then Packham's closed.

Two ambulancemen came running along the bank. They went straight over to Packham. One examined him and took his pulse, while the other assembled a canvas stretcher. They very carefully eased it under him, and then set off rapidly. The others followed in silence. By the time Jerry and Roly had hobbled back to the lane, the ambulance had gone and Mrs Packham had followed with Amelia. Mr Mills was amazed to see Roly, but very concerned about his cuts.

'We'll have to get him seen by a vet double-quick,' he said. The policeman offered to give them a lift home.

'I'll tell you what,' said Jerry's dad. 'You go on ahead, Cath, with Roly, in the police car and call the vet. I'll walk back with Jerry. I've something to tell him.'

So they went off in the car, Roly lying on a newspaper in the back.

'He'll be all right,' said Jerry's dad, as the car pulled away. 'They're clean cuts. But he's been in a fight, hasn't he?'

'Yes, Dad. He was in a fight with Brutus!' Briefly Jerry told his dad what he'd told Amelia.

'But why did you run off like that, Jerry?'

'I just couldn't stand it any longer, Dad. I'm sorry I worried you. But, please, don't let them send . . .'

136

'It's all right!' interrupted Mr Mills. 'That's what I wanted to tell you, son. We shan't have to. We're leaving!'

Jerry stopped and stared at him.

'Leaving??!'

'That's right. I've got another job. We had the interview yesterday. It's definite!' His father couldn't keep the excitement out of his voice.

'But where, Dad? What is it?'

'It's a caretaker at a National Trust place, a big house that's been turned into a museum. I'll be in charge of the gardens. There's a private part of the house that we'll live in. And no problem about pets. That's the first thing I asked!'

'Oh, Dad! . . . That's great.' Jerry felt like dancing, but his legs weren't up to it.

'I didn't want to tell you before, in case it fell through . . . but maybe I should have done. You've given me a hard time recently, Jerry. I started looking as soon as they sent Roly away, you know.' Jerry looked down.

'I didn't know, Dad . . . I'm sorry.'

'Well, I'm right sorry too. Maybe I should have told you. Let's shake on it anyhow.' With tears in his eyes, Jerry shook hands with his father. They set off again down the lane.

'I'll tell you something else,' said his dad, after a while. 'It's on the coast!' Jerry's eyes got big and round with excitement.

'Whereabouts?'

'It's a place called Salcombe. Down in Devon. It's about as far south as you can get, as a matter of fact.'

'Hey! The seaside. I'll be able to have a real boat. *Windrush the Second*!'

'Hang on,' laughed his dad. 'I didn't say anything about boats!'

When they got home the policeman was just leaving.

'I'm ever so sorry we've troubled you,' said Jerry's mum.

'Not at all,' he replied. 'If I hadn't been here, it would have taken longer to get an ambulance. Every minute counts in a case like that.'

'I hope they make it in time.'

'Well, we've done all we can. And more,' he added, looking at Jerry. 'Just don't go running off again without telling anyone where you're going, will you, son? Your folks deserve more than that. They think a lot of you . . . and I can see why. You probably saved that man's life today.' He patted Jerry on the shoulder, got in his car and drove off.

'Have you told him the news?' asked Jerry's mum.

'Of course I have. Didn't you notice? He's already doing his Long John Silver imitation?'

Jerry looked hurt. 'That wasn't my Long John Silver imitation, Dad,' he said. 'That was blisters!'

It was less than a week later that the removal van arrived at the Gatehouse. Mr Mills had offered to work a month's notice, but Mrs Packham had kindly said he might leave sooner if he wished. Captain Packham's horses were to be sold, so Wilf could take over the gardening. Captain Packham had suffered concussion and a stroke, as well as a broken arm. He was partly paralysed and couldn't speak properly, though the doctors hoped he would gradually improve. But it was clear he wouldn't ride again.

138

Jerry went next door with Roly to say goodbye to Wilf while they were loading up the van.

'So you're off, are you?' said Wilf. 'Well – I'm sorry to see you go. You brought a breath of fresh air to the place.'

'Why do you stay?' asked Jerry suddenly.

'Me?' He laughed, a little harshly. 'Where would I go, at my age? No . . . What it is, Jerry . . . I've sort of worked myself into the soil, like an old dock . . . Ha! you couldn't pull me up without breaking me . . . It seems to me that if you work a bit of ground long enough, you finish up belonging to it.'

Jerry frowned. 'But *it* doesn't belong to *you*.'

'Who says? What's "belong" mean? It's just a notion in your head . . . or a lawyer's scribble. Things is put here for us to take care of, and pass on . . . that's all there is to it. Any road, I reckon I belong here.'

'But what about . . . what you told me . . . you know, those people . . . Levellers?'

Wilf looked at him quizically. 'What about them?'

'About . . . you know, revolution . . . and sharing things out so everyone has the same amount.'

'Ah . . . said all that, did I? Well, Jerry, that's politics . . . and politics don't solve nothing in the end. You could have the most perfect set-up it was possible to invent, and folks'd bodge it up in a twelve-month.' He looked shrewdly at Jerry. 'No . . . it's people that have got to change, Jerry. They've got to fight that battle inside themselves, and win. It's not what you *have*, it's what you *give* that counts . . . Do you get me?'

Jerry nodded.

'I think so . . . Thanks for showing me all those things,'

he said.

'Well, that weren't nothing. But see you don't forget 'em. And don't go falling off any cliffs trying to get seagull's eggs!'

'I won't.' Just then Mrs Packham looked in at the door.

'Jerry. There you are!' she said. 'How stupid of me to call you Jamie all this time . . . you must have thought I was mad!'

'No . . . I didn't mind,' said Jerry. 'How is the Captain?'

'He's much better, thank you. His arm will be in plaster for months of course, but he can use his right hand . . . his speech may come back in time, they say. He understands what you did, and he wants me to thank you . . . and to give you this.'

She reached into her bag and took out the white cap with gold-braid worn by the rank of Captain. Jerry stared at it in amazement.

'It was his on his first command, in the war. It's quite funny really, you see, when he wrote "cap" I thought he wanted to wear it in hospital.' She gave a peal of laughter. 'I kept putting it on his head and he kept shaking it off – he got quite cross – anyway, he wrote that it was for you, and underlined it three times!'

Jerry took the cap. 'It's . . . it's great. Shall I try it on?'

'Certainly. It's yours.' It was rather too large. Wilf tilted it back a little.

'It suits you,' she said. 'You look very . . .'

'Jaunty,' said Wilf.

'That's the word!' she exclaimed. 'Positively jaunty.'

Without warning, something white shot up in front of Jerry, a paw flicked out and the cap went spinning through the air.

Wilf burst out laughing. Jerry bent to pick it up.

'I'm sorry, Mrs Packham,' he said. 'It's his only weakness, hats . . . and gloves.'

She gave another peal of laughter.

'I think it's because they make you look different' he went on. 'But I'll look after it. Say thanks to Captain Packham.'

'Of course . . . Oh, by the way, Amelia thought you might be coming up to say goodbye.'

Jerry looked down. 'Oh, could you say it for me . . . I've got to help load the van. Come on, pudding. Thanks again, Mrs Packham.'

'Come and visit us sometime,' she said.

'If I can. Cheerio, Wilf.'

'Cheerio, Captain,' he said. Jerry always remembered him standing there, raising his hand slowly in a solemn salute.

Amelia rode up on her horse just as they were leaving.

'Jerry,' she cried. 'Aren't you going to say goodbye?'

'Oh, yes. Goodbye.'

She dismounted hurriedly. 'Well, are you going to write?'

'I 'spect so.'

'But have you got my school address?'

'Yes, I wrote there before . . . don't you remember?' She flushed. 'I'll send you a card,' he added. 'From the seaside.'

The house was finely placed on a headland overlooking the mouth of the estuary. The wealthy and eccentric owner had spent his life making huge collections of butterflies, moths,

141

beetles, stuffed animals, fossils and photographs, and left everything to the National Trust in his will.

The gardens were the most beautiful Jerry had ever seen: small velvety lawns set at different levels on the steep hillside, connected by winding rocky paths enclosed by rare shrubs and tall mature trees. In the topmost garden was a bronze statue of a lady. She was in the act of releasing birds, one arm flung high above her head. From this lovely arbour a path led out along the cliffs.

Jerry had followed this path and was sitting on the cliff-top, watching a pair of ravens tumbling like acrobats and smelling the coconut-scented gorse. Roly was lying beside him eyeing the Captain's cap, which Jerry turned over and over absently in his hands. Roly's coat was white and glossy again. All the cuts had healed, leaving only faint scars on his belly.

Jerry looked towards the little town of Salcombe, huddled round the harbour. Jumbled old roofs, white and pink cottages, a couple of hotels. And the people . . . just fishermen, shopkeepers, nothing grand – except the sea. He put on his captain's cap and squinted down the estuary and out across the miles of glittering, ownerless water.

'Yes, Roly,' he said. 'I think we're going to like it here.'

A paw darted out. The cap spun into the air, and a sudden gust of wind sent it sailing out over the cliff-top. Jerry sprang to his feet.

'Oh no! It's gone!' The white and gold cap skimmed and flashed out in a great arc, twisting and wheeling like a bird, as it dwindled and was finally lost amongst the spangles of sunlight dancing on the surface of the sea.

'Never mind, Roly' said Jerry. 'Maybe it belongs there.'

The End

Do not be troubled, God, though they say 'mine'
of all things that permit it patiently.
They are like wind that lightly strokes the boughs
and says: MY tree.

They hardly see
how all things glow that their hands seize upon,
so that they cannot touch
even the utmost fringe and not be singed.

They will say 'mine' as one will sometimes call
the prince his friend in speech with villagers,
this prince being very great – and far away.
They call strange walls 'mine', knowing not at all
who is the master of the house indeed.
They still say 'mine', and claim possession, though
each thing, as they approach, withdraws and closes;
a silly charlatan perhaps thus poses
as owner of the lightning and the sun.
And so they say: my life, my wife, my child,
my dog, well knowing all that they have styled
their own: life, wife, child, dog, remain
shapes alien and unknown,
that blindly groping they must stumble on.
This truth, be sure, only the great discern,
who long for eyes.

Rainer Maria Rilke